Holiday Love 1

Season of Kneading Love

PROSE & CONCEPTS

NADIA HAN

To those "kneading" the best buns.

·

·

·

"Hold fast to dreams, for if dreams die, life is a broken-winged bird that cannot fly."

— Langston Hughes

COPYRIGHT

Season of Kneading Love

Copyright © 2025 by Nadia Han

Cover Art Copyright: Nadia Han

Editor: Anna Nesbitt

Proofreaders: Partners in Crime Book Services

First edition Ebook ISBN: 978-1-952820-76-2

First edition Paperback ISBN: 978-1-952820-77-9

CHAPTER ONE

AVA

BLACK FRIDAY WAS a monster that smiled every single November when people fed it money. Until this year, I never shopped on this day. I made an exception for my mom, who just completed chemo. She had been diagnosed with breast cancer over a year ago and just finished her treatment. Wanting to celebrate and make her smile, I braved this crazy day to buy her a Christmas gift.

As expected, the mall was packed. I should've placed the order online, but I feared they'd run out of the limited edition teardrop emerald bracelet with a 14K gold chain. A month ago, my mom's face lit up when she saw the commercial for it on TV. *That's gorgeous. I've never seen a bracelet like that.*

My mom wore little jewelry, but not because she didn't like it. She was pragmatic. As a single parent, she'd worked two jobs to provide for me after my father died in a car accident when I was ten. She understood the need to spend only on necessities. Even though she didn't need to work so hard anymore, she was used to saving money instead of spending it.

It was time she got what she deserved—beautiful jewelry that reflected her character. Emeralds.

My heart sank looking at the jam-packed parking lot at the mall. Praying, I drove around and gasped when I saw a white SUV reversing out of a parking spot. I sped up and turned on my blinker. But as soon as the SUV left, a black sedan with too many bumper stickers snuck in, stealing my spot.

I slammed on my horn, rolled down the window, and shouted, "I was waiting for that spot!"

A burly man exited the car with his friend, who wore a dark hooded sweatshirt.

"We were here first, Mark." The bulky man turned to his friend.

"Yeah. You were too late." Mark laughed as he strode away with the burly man.

Fuming, I shouted, "Liar! I was waiting first!"

Why are people so obnoxious?

Anger surged as several scenarios popped into my head. I wished I had a carton of eggs to decorate his car. I wished I had a knife to slash his tires. *Ugh, I hate this feeling.* I closed my eyes and breathed, trying to calm my anger.

Someone knocked on the back window of my car. I jerked and opened my eyes. An old woman with a friendly face walked up to me with a teenage girl beside her. I rolled down the window.

"Ignore those jerks," said the old woman, wearing a gray coat with a red scarf. "We're leaving. Do you want our spot?"

"Yes, please!" Hope burst in me.

"I'll stand off to the side to make sure you get the spot,"

said the teenager, wearing a white knit hat. "Grandma saw what those men did to you. They suck."

"Thank you."

After I parked and turned off the engine, I sat for a moment, appreciating the kind people who gave me hope. Good people made the terrible moments sting less.

Shoving the irritation aside, I rushed into the mall and maneuvered my way through the crowds of shoppers. Holiday music blasted around me. The scents of cinnamon, pine, and vanilla swarmed me as I passed a candle store where two sales associates offered discount coupons. I took one and said I'd return later. A girl could never have enough scented candles.

As I headed toward Artisan Jewelers, I glanced up at the second level of the mall, and my chest tightened. A man walked with a woman in a wool coat. Was that my ex, Austin Tanner? My pace slowed as I studied the couple. When he turned toward my direction, it was clear he wasn't my ex, a coward who didn't have the courage to end our relationship respectfully.

It had been over a year since he dumped me via text. We'd been together for two years before that fateful day when my heart died.

Forget about him.

I blew out a heavy breath and entered Artisan Jewelers. So many people browsed the store. The combination of crowds, scents of candles, perfumes, colognes, and chaotic energy made it difficult for me to focus on jewelry. Despite that, I walked up to the counter and looked into the display case.

"Can I help you?" asked a lady wearing a poinsettia pin on her black dress and the nametag Jessica.

"Yes, Jessica. I'm looking for the teardrop emerald bracelet." I pointed to the tall banner promoting it.

"We have only two left in stock." Her blue eyes beamed. "More are coming next week. I'll be right back."

When she brought it over from another counter, I examined the bracelet. "It's so pretty."

"It really is." She smiled as a coworker called out to her. "Just a moment." She stepped over to the nearby counter.

I stepped to the corner as more people approached the counter. A musky men's fragrance snuck into my nose, and I sneezed into my coat's sleeve. I glanced up, looking for a familiar face. But I only saw an unfamiliar man looking at the glass counter with his significant other. The cologne was like Austin's, but slightly different.

I had to cleanse myself of Austin. I'd tried, but little things kept reminding me of him. Maybe I needed to go ask my friend, Rhea, to use her palo santo on me. She worked at Serenity Wellness, a metaphysical store that offered alternative healing, crystals and tarot readings.

Turning my focus back to the bracelet, I studied the teardrop cut. My mom's birthday was in May, and emerald was her birthstone. Mine was peridot, another green birthstone representing August.

On the counter was a pamphlet with the various stones and their attributes. I picked it up and read that emeralds symbolized fertility, rebirth, nature, and the cycle of life. The calming energy of emeralds helped release emotional blockages to foster inner peace. It also enhanced intuition.

The stone described my mom perfectly. I admired how she handled the terrifying ordeal with ease and grace. Her acceptance of the inevitability of death gave me inner strength, soothing me at a time when I should have been soothing her.

As for the peridot, which was a bright yellow-green, it symbolized harmony, peace, luck, and comfort—all the things I wanted for my life. The vibrant green promoted general wellness.

But in the past year, I couldn't believe in those things.

Don't let one man ruin your outlook.

Jessica returned and grinned. "Would you like me to wrap it up?"

"Yes, please."

After paying for the expensive bracelet, I tucked the velvet jewelry box into my purse and walked back to the candle store to browse. I picked up the Warm Sugar Cookies and Cedarwood candles, inhaling each one. These aromas made me feel cozy.

"Don't forget to use your coupon! It's only for today!" cheered the sales associate wearing a Santa hat.

I could get my friends candles this year for our little gathering. Kendra Hoang, Rhea Summers, Layla Kwan, Jemma Lopez, and Deidre Florakis didn't spend lavishly on our gift exchange. We just liked our ritual holiday gathering to catch up with each other. After the sales associate wrapped the candles safely and placed them into a bag, I glanced at my watch. I could pick up lunch before heading home.

As I walked out of the candle store, a group of people swarmed the associate giving away discount coupons. I stepped forward but stopped when two women with multiple shopping bags almost crashed into me.

"Sorry!" said the woman carrying four bags. "It's crazy here today."

"It's okay." I stepped off to the side and stared at the jam-packed mall, trying to see where I could squeeze through.

I never saw the mall this crowded. The irresistible sales brought out more people than I anticipated.

That musky scent hit me again, causing me to sneeze. Someone bumped into me and apologized. I couldn't tell who it was as people pushed past me. I didn't want to linger around because I'd spend more money on things I didn't need. My mom's gift had already taken a chunk out of my depleting savings.

I headed to the parking lot, glancing around to see if there was a car looking for a spot. No one was around. *Oh well.* I would have liked to offer my spot to someone. I walked toward my car when I sensed someone close to me. I turned and almost bumped into a man wearing a black, hooded coat. Fear twisted in my stomach as he smirked and yanked at the body of my purse, but I gripped it tightly, creating a tug-of-war.

"Let go!" he snarled.

"Help me!" I screamed and whacked my bag of candles at his face. Something cracked, and blood gushed from his nose.

He shoved me to the ground. Snatching my purse, he ran but tripped on something. He braced a hand on the ground as the contents inside the purse scattered everywhere. Then he pushed himself up, lunging toward me.

"Someone help me!" I shouted again.

Then voices boomed. "Are you okay, miss?"

The man ran off as a friendly couple rushed over to help me get up. They gathered up the candles and stuffed them back into the bag. Thank goodness for the bubble wrap around each candle. I gathered the items dispersed from my purse and gasped when I didn't see the velvet jewelry box.

"Did you see a green velvet box?" I asked the couple.

"No, did he take it?" asked the woman in the furry coat.

Terror and adrenaline muddled my mind and speech, so I nodded.

"Peter, call the police," said the woman, who introduced herself as Patty.

"Thank you, Patty and Peter, I'm Ava."

"You're welcome. I hope they'll catch him soon!" Patty huffed.

My body shook with fear and anger. I glanced around, but the thief could have been anywhere by now. He probably snatched the jewelry during the scuffle. I should have been more careful.

Minutes later, the police arrived and took my statement, including the couple's. The only details I remembered about the Caucasian man were that he wore a black coat and a black hat. I thought I saw some blond hair sticking out from his hat. He was about six feet tall. Other than that, I couldn't remember anything. Everything happened so fast.

"Don't stress. If you remember anything else, call me." Officer Jensen scribbled a number on a piece of paper for me. "I'll browse the parking lot and check out the cameras from security. I'll let you know if I uncover anything."

"Thank you," I said.

Officer Jensen returned to his cruiser and made a call.

A Lexus SUV pulled up with Austin in the driver's seat, looking right at me. My heart galloped as he stepped out, walking straight toward me.

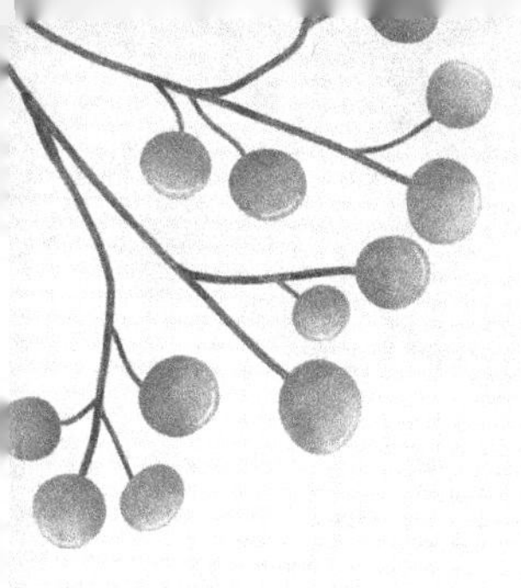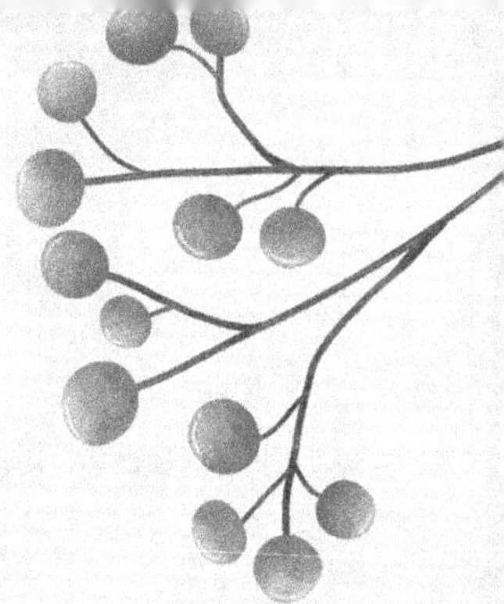

CHAPTER TWO

AUSTIN

I HADN'T BEEN to the mall in years, and I couldn't believe my eyes when I saw Ava. She appeared distraught. Why was a police car there?

"Hey," I said, trying my best to calm my racing heart. "Are you okay?"

"What are you doing here?" she asked, taking one step back from me.

Pain squeezed my heart. *It's your own fault, asshole.*

"Picking up an order for my mother. What happened here?" I gestured to the police car with flashing lights.

Ava stared at me with those big brown eyes I remembered so well. Curiosity, confusion, and anger flashed in them.

"Why do you care?" she asked coldly.

"She fought off a thief." A woman in a furry coat placed a hand on Ava's back. "The police will find him, sweetheart. We've got to go now."

"Thank you for helping me." Ava smiled at the couple. "Happy Holidays."

"Same to you." The couple walked off.

Protectiveness soared in me. "What does he look like? Where is he?"

"That's not your business." Ava turned and walked toward her car.

My fingers curled, wanting to yank her back into my arms. But that wouldn't happen. She hated me and with good reason. No respectable man ends a perfect relationship via text.

I watched her drive off and my chest tightened. As I walked back to my car, a police officer exited his cruiser. I recognized a family friend I hadn't seen in a while.

Jeremy Jensen saw me, saluted, and walked over.

"How's it going?" He shook my hand. "Christmas shopping?"

"Not really. Just running an errand for my mother. What happened here?"

"We have a thief on the loose. It's not surprising at this time of the year. But he did it in broad daylight. The woman whacked him in the head with some candles."

I smiled, remembering her stubbornness. I didn't see any injuries on Ava just now. But what if the asshole had done something to her? My body shivered at the dark scenario.

"Was she hurt?" I asked.

"No." Jeremy glanced around. "I'm meeting the mall security to check their cameras. The thief took a bracelet from her."

As I drove home, thoughts about texting her swirled within me. Was she feeling better? What had she been up to? I tried to follow her social media accounts for the past year, but she rarely posted on them.

Stop it.

I should let her move on. I was the one who broke things off. Despite that, I couldn't move on from Ava. No man could move on after being with her. Just *look* at her—beautiful and strong. She consumed me through and through.

Arriving home, I pulled into my car garage, and my phone rang. I wasn't in the mood to talk to Sierra, my ex-fiancée. But if I didn't pick up, my phone would continue ringing.

"Hi Sierra." I entered my kitchen.

"Austin, my love. Have you thought things over?"

I pinched the space between my eyebrows, trying to ease the tension. Concern for Ava and irritation with Sierra stirred in me. Sierra should move on. There were no emotions between us. Our arranged engagement lasted one month. It took me that month to convince my father I'd never go along with his insane idea. Thinking about the situation increased my blood pressure, so I shoved it away.

"There's nothing to think about, Sierra. There's nothing between us."

"You're wrong about that. I've always wanted you. That's why I asked my father to propose the engagement. We're perfect for each other, Austin. My family can help your family."

Frustration boiled inside me. "So it was your idea for the engagement?"

"You're better off with me than your ex, who works for the city. She can't help you." Sierra sighed as though she were losing her patience with me. "My father knew I wanted you, so he helped me. I always get what I want."

Sierra Montage was the epitome of a privileged woman who didn't want to accept anything that went against her needs. A spoiled brat who kept being spoiled.

"There's nothing wrong with a city job. Ava is excellent at what she does," I said between clenched teeth. "We are done, Sierra. Accept it. Move on, because I have."

"You have? Who is she?" she demanded.

"That's not important. What's important is that you need to stop contacting me." I strode over to the medicine cabinet, popped two painkillers into my mouth, and gulped them down with a glass of water. "Ask your father to arrange a relationship with a man who's interested. I've got to go."

I hung up, walked over to the living room, and dropped onto the couch. Sierra didn't have to work—would never have to work for the rest of her life. Everything was provided for her. Ava worked hard toward her dreams. I felt honored that she once shared them with me.

I take Ava's hands in mine as we walk down a retail strip with a flower shop, pet store, hair salon, and a coffee shop.

"That apple tart looks delicious." She drags me into the bakery. We buy coffee, an apple tart, and an almond croissant. She breaks off a piece of the apple tart and feeds me. "What do you think?"

I shrug. "Okay."

Then she bites a piece and sighs. "What do you mean? It's delicious."

"Your sweet bread is better."

She smiles, and my heart swells. "You're only saying that because I'm your girlfriend and you get free bread from me."

I laugh. "Having a talented girlfriend who can make heavenly bread is a perk. But seriously, your bread and pastries are amazing! Everyone who has tried them agrees. Remember that time you made a tray of animal-shaped breads for me to bring to my meeting?"

She grins. "They were fun to make."

"People loved the bunny breads. They wanted to place orders, but you didn't have time to make them."

She leans into me, and her floral perfume makes me want to take her back to my place and devour her.

"I've been saving money to open a small bakery," she says. "No one knows about this but you. So keep it mum, okay?" She places a finger on my lips.

I grip her finger and kiss it. "How much do you need? I can help."

Her face brightens. "No. Save your money to help your family business. But thanks."

I loved that she cared about my family's real estate business. At that time, Tanner Properties suffered multiple losses because my father made some awful investments. I had promised myself once I got my business back on track, I'd help Ava attain her dream.

Would she accept my help now? Based on the disdain on her face earlier today, I'd say she wanted to stay far away from me. I deserved it.

Tell her the truth.

I scrubbed a hand down my face, wondering if I'd ever resolve this predicament. I'd asked for a chance to explain, but she ignored all my voicemails, text messages, and emails. Would she want to hear my explanation now?

CHAPTER THREE

AVA

ANNOYANCE AND WORRY clung to me as I entered my condo. Why couldn't I shake him off?

It had been over a year since we broke up. My body shouldn't have this reaction to him. When he stood close to me, I wanted to fall into his protective arms that used to make me feel safe. Though my body remembered the comfort, I remembered the pain that chopped up my heart.

How had I not known about him and Sierra? I always thought I had good intuition, so what happened? I should've sensed something.

Love blinds people.

How could he have been engaged to a crazed woman like Sierra Montage? Last year, she was accused of burning down a woman's house for dating her ex-boyfriend. She also slashed her ex's tires while he was at work. Somehow she got away with the crimes. Her family probably paid off people or threatened them. Money talked. Maybe that was what Austin wanted. But then why had he ended the engagement a month after it was announced?

Maybe I needed a few more years to truly expunge him from my body and mind. He was like an illness that lingered and flared up with certain triggers. Today's trigger was seeing his concern for me. It didn't seem fake, but it made me angry.

Why care about me when you've hurt me so badly?

I hopped into the shower, hoping the warm water would wash the thoughts of him away. I let the steamy water soothe me when the thief popped into my vision. Would the police recover the bracelet in time? I doubted it.

I had to buy another bracelet for my mother, but finances were tight. A pipe burst in my kitchen last month, and my car needed new tires and brakes. These necessities took an enormous chunk of money from my savings. The dream of my little bakery dwindled before my eyes. Maybe this was a sign from the universe telling me to give it up.

Sadness gripped my heart. My dad was a baker, and he worked for a well-known bakery in Shrewsbury. His dream was to open a bakery one day, so he could share his creativity with the community, but he never got that chance. I fell in love with baking because of my dad. Opening a shop was my dream—to explore my creativity and honor him. But now that might not happen.

Sadness swelled in my chest like dough. I had to do something about the situation. I had little left in my savings, but I wanted to get my mom the bracelet.

As an admin assistant for the Department of Public Works for the City of Worcester, I didn't make a lot of money. But I enjoyed serving the community. The pension the city offered was security for my retirement. I needed to find a part-time job to supplement the bracelet and other emergencies that could pop up.

Some comfy pajamas put me in a better mood. I could look for a part-time job during my lunch break at work. After making chamomile tea, I sat down to watch the news, mostly for the weather.

"Authorities are searching for a man responsible for stealing multiple items from the Solomon Pond Mall today," said the reporter with red lipstick that matched her shirt. She listed items including my bracelet. Apparently, the same thief stole a pair of diamond earrings and a watch hours after my incident.

How brazen!

"The police believe the suspect has help. If you recognize this man or know anything about this case, please call the number below. The holidays are upon us. Be careful when you do your holiday shopping."

I prayed they'd catch the thief soon so people could be at ease. The holidays were filled with magic. That magical feeling was like spring when I felt hopeful. I grabbed my phone and sent a text to my group chat.

Ava: *Be careful when you shop.*

Rhea: *I saw the news.*

Kendra: *What's wrong with people?*

Layla: *Lots of things.*

Ava: *He stole my bracelet.* ☹

Rhea: *What? The gift for your mom?*

Ava: *Yeah.*

Kendra: *I hope he catches a nasty disease.*

Jemma: *People are jerks!*

Ava: *If you know of a part-time job, let me know.*

Rhea: *Why?*

Ava: *Gonna replace the bracelet. It's expensive.*

All my friends agreed to let me know. Then we finalized the date for our holiday gathering.

I didn't tell them I'd encountered Austin. They'd swarm me with questions, and I didn't want to think about him right now. My body was just calming down from the resurgence of feelings he elicited.

Snuggling into my bed, I shifted my lavender-scented candle aside to make room for my phone to charge. The soothing aroma reminded me of the musky cologne from the mall. It was similar to what Austin wore. But I'd never sneezed when I was around him.

I'd smelled this scent when I was in the jewelry store and when I bought candles. Could they be the same person? Many people wore that cologne, including Austin.

Revelation dawned on me. The man who had snatched my purse didn't wear this cologne. I didn't remember sneezing. If he didn't take the emerald bracelet, then who did? I replayed that chaotic day through my head. A skilled thief could've taken the jewelry box when I was still inside the mall. Numerous people had bumped into me. It could've been anyone.

I could rule Austin out of the theft equation. From what I gathered, Tanner Properties had expanded, which meant he was doing well. He didn't need to steal my emerald bracelet. He could buy Sierra all the jewelry she wanted. Though their engagement had ended, she still posted about them on her social media posts as though they were still together.

My phone pinged with a text. Thinking it was one of my friends, I reached for it, and my heart galloped.

Why was Austin texting me?

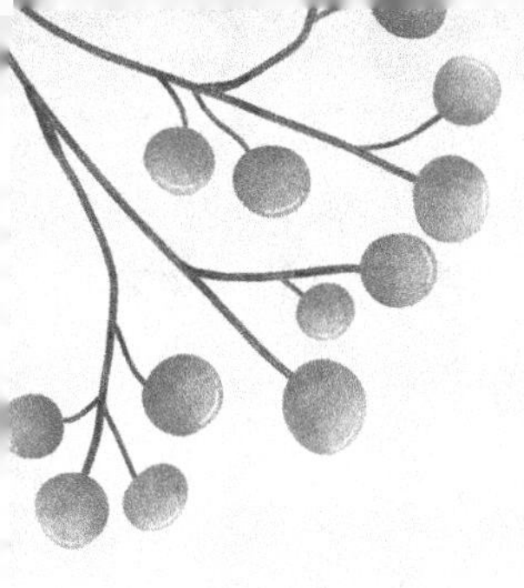
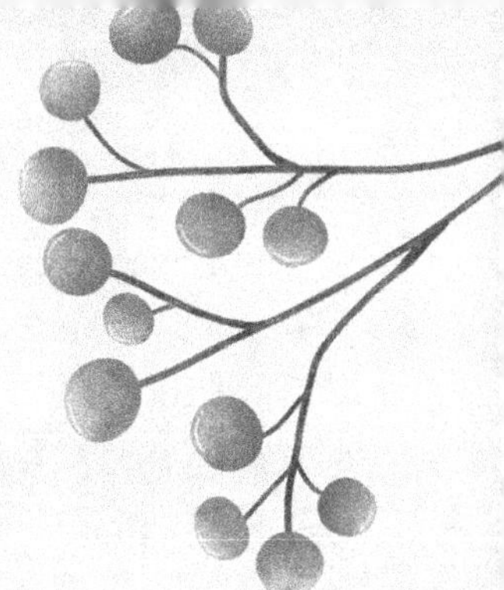

CHAPTER FOUR

AUSTIN

I WASN'T sure if my intuition served me well, but I had to know if Ava was all right. Her distraught look still worried me.

Austin: *How are you?*

I saw she read my message, but I wasn't sure if she'd reply.

My heart hammered when I saw the three dots moving on the screen.

Ava: *Why?*

My fingers curled, unsure of how to reply. After a moment, she responded.

Ava: *I'm okay. Thanks for asking.*

Austin: *Be careful when you go shopping.*

She didn't reply.

Austin: *I'm sorry about the past. I hope we can be friends when we see each other again.*

Three dots appeared, then they disappeared.

Ava: *Friends? That would be hard.*

Those words knifed me in the chest. But what did I expect?

I didn't know how to reply to her. What if I said the wrong thing? It wasn't a good idea to contact her tonight.

My phone rang, and I was glad for the distraction.

"Hi, Bianca. Is everything going well?"

Bianca was my new business's manager.

"Our baker, Paula, got into a terrible car accident."

"Oh no. Is she okay?" I asked.

A friend had referred Paula to me. She made the best cupcakes.

"She'll be out for a few weeks."

Today was a day that delivered unlimited bad news.

"Don't worry. Rhea says she knows someone perfect to help until Paula returns."

Rhea was Bianca's younger sister.

"Okay, great. Keep me posted. If we need to hire more employees for this busy season, just let me know."

"Will do."

CHAPTER FIVE

AVA

THE DAY FLEW by at work with several meetings and people calling about missed trash pickups, recycling bin replacements, and residential salt and sand distribution. My mom called during lunch, saying her friend Julie was visiting from Maine for a week. Julie knew what Mom was going through because she survived breast cancer three years ago. The friendly support would help my mom recover even faster.

A text from Rhea popped onto my phone during work, but I didn't have time to reply until I got home.

Rhea: *Call me.*

My stomach growled, and I grabbed a leftover chicken lo mein in my microwaveable container to heat up.

While waiting, I called Rhea, and she picked up right away. "Hey, you!"

"Sorry, I couldn't call earlier. What's up?" I grabbed a fork and poured myself a glass of water, placing them on the kitchen table.

"I have the perfect part-time job for you!" Excitement filled her voice.

"Really?" Something tickled my stomach as I got my heated food, brought it over to the kitchen table, and sat down. "Where?"

"Bianca manages No Name Bakery. The main baker got into a car accident and needs to be out of work for a few weeks. They need someone to replace her quickly."

"I thought she worked for Maplegrove Bread Company? Besides, I haven't worked in a bakery before."

"She wanted a change—something not so corporate," Rhea said. "You bake at home all the time. Your pastries—especially your *bread*—are to die for. You'd be perfect. Bianca has been in the industry for a long time, so she can spot talent. And she said you've got it."

"She did?" I smiled at the compliment.

I knew I could do it, but my inexperience working for a real bakery made me uncomfortable. What if I made a mistake that cost them money? What if I messed up and no one wanted to eat my products?

Go for it! Kick self-doubt to the curb!

The image of the emerald bracelet flashed in front of me, and I gathered courage. This experience was a test to see if I could attain my dream of opening my own bakery one day. No Name was a fabulous opportunity to gain experience.

"Okay. I'll do it."

"Fantastic! I'll let her know. She'll call you for more details."

We ended the call, and I finished my dinner while eagerness soared through me. My fingers itched as though they knew they'd be playing with dough, sugar, other fun ingredients, and baking tools.

As I prepared my lunch for tomorrow, Bianca called to let me know she'd send over the employment form for me to fill out. We'd start with me working three days a week after my day job and full days on the weekends. I'd be working for No Name for three weeks with the potential for me to stay longer if I wanted to.

"Why is it called No Name?" I asked.

"I asked the same question." She laughed. "The owner didn't know what to call it. The pay is good. There are three other coworkers. Cindy will assist you in the kitchen. I'll help as well, but I'll be more focused on day-to-day operations, admin stuff, and fulfilling the holiday orders."

"Do you have a lot?"

"We have a good amount. If you make your animal-shaped breads, we'll have way more."

"You'd let me make them?" My heart raced.

"Absolutely! I'd like you to bring your version of bread and pastries to the mix. People will love it."

After our chat, I felt more at ease. I looked at my calendar and drew hearts on the days I'd be at the bakery. That night, I fell asleep dreaming of bread in all shapes and sizes. Adorable elf- and gnome-shaped breads came to life, helping me decorate No Name Bakery. They even moved the letters of the name around, creating a new title that didn't make sense.

CHAPTER SIX

AVA

I WOKE up at three in the morning eager to start my first Saturday at No Name. The past three evenings were incredible. The joy that burst in my heart as I kneaded dough for my bunny bread was indescribable. Working there was better than I imagined. I didn't know why I was fearful at first. *Silly me.*

I washed up, dressed in dark cotton pants and threw on a long-sleeve knit top. I'd be spending most of my time in the back fulfilling orders for my bunny-shaped sweet bread. As Bianca had predicted, they were a big hit. The bakery's social media page got a surge of followers after I posted images of my adorable bread, which went viral.

It was 3:30 a.m. when I left my house. Cindy, the assistant baker, started at 2:00 a.m. I should be tired, but enthusiasm coursed through me. I couldn't wait for people to buy my bread and pastries.

As I drove my Honda Civic in toward the bakery, which was in the lovely business area on the west side of the city, my chest constricted. I thought back to a time when I had walked around this area dreaming about my shop. Some shops had moved out for new ones to come in.

Working for No Name was indirectly living my dream. I got to do what I loved and didn't have to worry about the other details required to run a business. This gig wasn't bad at all. I smiled as I pulled into the on-street parking spot behind Cindy's car. We saved the small parking lot for customers.

My life was slowly getting back on track. The passion for my dream was renewed. Hope filled my heart, and I was grateful for the opportunity to work with dedicated coworkers.

I walked into the back room and grinned. "Morning, Cindy!"

In her early forties, she wore a net around her curly brown hair and a red apron with her name embroidered on it. She was married to her high school sweetheart, who worked as a mechanic.

"Good morning to you! Coffee is ready." She smiled and gestured to the pot.

"Thanks." I poured myself a cup, twisted my hair into a low bun, pulled a net over my hair, tossed on my apron, and got to work.

Cindy prepared the donuts, muffins, and danishes while I got out the dough I'd prepped last night. Soft holiday music played in the background as we worked. It was nice knowing the city was asleep while you prepared their meals.

Before I knew it, Bianca arrived with Rosie Renken and Donna Russo, signifying it was six in the morning. Bianca was married with twin girls, so I could see why she wanted something different from her stressful corporate job.

"Ready to seize the day?" she asked everyone as she tied her red hair into a ponytail.

"You betcha!" Rosie cheered. She was in her late fifties and with cheeks that matched her name. Her husband worked in HR at Worcester State University.

Donna offered me a one-armed hug. "You're still here? We didn't scare you away?"

I laughed. "Not yet."

Donna had three grandchildren, but you wouldn't know looking at her flawless skin. In her sixties, she worked part time as well and lived two blocks away.

When the shop opened at 7:30 a.m., time flew by. We kept restocking everything. When 10:00 a.m. arrived, my stomach growled. I grabbed a turkey sandwich Bianca made and sat in the lunchroom to eat. Suddenly, tingles skipped down my spine, making my body fully aware someone was nearby.

His deep voice sounded, and the muscles in my stomach contorted as though it were making pretzels.

"Morning, everyone!" Austin said.

What was he doing here? I grabbed my bottle of water and sipped. Was he a VIP customer coming to pick up an order? Or was he stalking me?

"Hi, boss!" Bianca exclaimed. "You're early."

Boss? Austin owned No Name Bakery? My heart thundered as I tried to find a place to hide.

Don't be ridiculous.

Why would he own a bakery? How had I not known about this?

This was so awkward, especially after our text messages after the theft incident. Though I couldn't be friends with my exes, I could be friendly. I *had* to be if I wanted to keep this job. I needed the money for my mom's bracelet.

I inhaled and exhaled, trying my best to calm myself. Of all the surprises I'd encountered recently, this had to take the prize.

"I heard the bunny bread is selling like hotcakes," he said. "Where's the baker?"

Ugh.

"She's in the lunchroom," Bianca said as Donna called her for assistance.

"Go take care of the customer. I know where the lunchroom is."

Footsteps approached, and nerves churned even more. I glanced at the storage closet. How long could I hide in there before Bianca started looking for me? I cursed myself for the pathetic idea. Why should I be afraid of him? I had nothing to be ashamed of.

He made you feel unworthy.

The admission stopped my breath. I was a confident woman, so I shouldn't let a man determine my worth. His breakup had shattered my heart and belief in myself. The unexpected blow hurt me to the core. I thought we had something special—something solid and unshakeable. But he left me for a woman with status and influence.

I rose, getting ready to leave when he stepped into the room, wearing a three-quarter length wool coat and dark pants. His presence took the air out of the room. Or maybe it was me not being able to breathe properly.

"Hi." Austin smiled, the blue in his eyes sparkled. Nothing had changed on his handsome face, except the lines between his eyebrows had deepened.

"Hello," I said, trying to be courteous to my *boss*. "You own this bakery?"

He nodded, studying me. Heat bloomed all over my body.

Stop staring at me.

When he didn't reply, I asked. "Why? You don't have enough to do at Tanner Properties?"

"I do." A smirk crept onto his lips. "But this is a passion project of mine."

I wanted to ask so many questions, but it wasn't my business. Apparently, I didn't know him at all. I dated a stranger for two years. He'd been in love with another woman while he was dating me. He had a passion project I didn't know about. I'd been so blind and stupid.

He probably saw something in my eyes and said, "Bianca tells me your bread is a big hit. I'm glad you're here."

I didn't know how to reply. My mother taught me courtesy never hurts anyone.

"Thank you." I walked over toward the trash bin, slipped on something on the floor, and fell backwards.

Austin caught me, but he also slipped. We both toppled onto the kitchen tiles, with him holding on to me, making sure I was on top of him.

"Are you okay?" he asked as his warm breath tickled my ear.

The musky cologne snuck up my nose. I didn't sneeze. The scent took on a distinct scent when it was on him.

"Yes. You?" I pushed myself up and looked at the wet floor and followed the trail. "Oh no, the sink's leaking."

He got up and winced, rubbing his shoulder.

"Are you hurt?" I asked.

"I'll be okay." He reached into his coat, pulled out his phone, and called someone I assumed was the plumber.

It would've been my shoulder in pain if he hadn't taken the brunt of it.

I mopped the floor while he spoke on the phone. When his call ended, he took off his coat, got under the sink, and turned off the water.

Getting up, he rolled his right shoulder. "Jack will be here soon."

"Do you need some painkillers?" I walked up to him. "I've got some in my purse."

Energy thrummed between us. I didn't realize I stood so close to him. For a moment, time stopped, and the pain and resentment from the past faded into the background. All I saw was the man who encouraged me to go after my dreams. His eyes held mine, and I saw pain and something else in them.

He lifted his hand and brushed it down my cheek, and heat blossomed on contact. The muscles in my inner thighs flexed. I broke the trance and stepped back.

"Sure, I'll take some painkillers," he said.

When I dropped them into his palm, he asked, "Can we chat?"

"Why?" I asked.

"Don't you want to know what happened over a year ago?"

"I know what happened, Austin." Anger surged. "You dumped me via text."

His eyebrows pushed together as he opened his mouth to say something, but Bianca interrupted, "Jack is here." She looked at me. "What happened?"

I pointed to the sink and was grateful for the interruption. When my shift ended, I walked out to my car. Austin stood in front of the shop on his phone. He saw me and waved. I returned the gesture, got into my car, and drove off. In the rearview mirror, I saw him looking in my direction.

Deep down, I wanted to know if our relationship had been a lie. Did he care for me at all?

I loved him. Tears rolled down my face, blurring my vision. I loved a man who didn't love me. That revelation shattered me. If I hadn't loved him, it would've been easier to move on.

Hear him out.

Perhaps that would help me move on once and for all.

CHAPTER SEVEN

AVA

FIVE MINUTES after I put on my apron at No Name Bakery, Austin walked into the kitchen, startling me and Cindy. He wore a dark puffy coat and jeans, looking like a model for some fashion magazine. His hair was a perfect mess, reminding me of when I used to run my fingers through it. It should be illegal for anyone to look this gorgeous.

Cindy and I exchanged curious glances.

What was he doing here at the butt crack of dawn? Wealthy men like him didn't need to start their day this early. Even if they did, they'd be on their computers in the comfort of their home office. The plumber fixed the leak already, so he couldn't be here checking on it.

"Morning!" He smiled as though he'd been up for hours. His eyes slid over to me and stayed. Heat bloomed all over me.

"Morning to you too." Cindy waved. "Is there a meeting we don't know about?"

"No meeting." He took off his coat, hung it on the hook

on the wall, and walked up to our table. "I want the baker's experience." He looked at me. "Teach me?"

My mouth dropped open. He should direct that question to Cindy, who had been his employee far longer than I had.

What was Austin trying to do?

Cindy looked at me, then him. "Sure! Grab an apron from the wall." She pointed to where all the aprons hung next to a rack of bowls.

Austin pulled on a green apron and stood next to Cindy. He watched and listened intently to her demonstration of pouring batter into the muffin mold. From across the table, I studied him as I prepared my bread, for which I had to double the recipe. The shop sold out of my sweet bunny bread yesterday.

Austin looked over and met my eyes. "Once I graduate from Cindy's training, I'm heading to yours."

Cindy laughed, and I smiled.

When the rest of the crew arrived, all were surprised to see Austin in the kitchen. Everyone got to work, and the hours flew by. I knew the shop was crowded from all the customer chatter that traveled back into the kitchen. Cindy ran out to help Bianca, Rosie, and Donna, leaving me with Austin. My body became aware of his presence.

"Business has been great since you started." Austin stepped over to my table, standing beside me. A smear of batter clung to the side of his chin.

Should I tell him? Or should I be naughty and leave it?

Though a part of me wanted to embarrass him, the better side of me knew I'd want someone to tell me if I had something unattractive on my face.

"You have a smear on your face." I tapped my chin.

"Where?" He touched his forehead, cheek, nose, and neck, missing the smear on his chin.

"Right here." I wiped the batter from his chin with my finger. "See?"

"Oh, thanks." A smirk flashed onto his lips before I cleaned the dough off my finger.

I narrowed my eyes at him, and a silent conversation exchanged between us. This was what we used to do. We just had to look at each other and know what the other was thinking. I'd never been able to read anyone the way I could him. More so, no one had been able to read me the way he could.

Ava: *You did that on purpose.*

Austin: *Did what?*

Ava: *Pretend you didn't know where the smear was.*

Austin: *Don't know what you're talking about.*

"I'm ready to learn from the best." He flexed his fingers, changing the subject.

We both knew what had just occurred. Despite that, an icicle in my heart melted a little. Was I being too soft on him? I still hadn't answered him regarding his explanation. Yes, I wanted to know everything. But I feared it would drag me through hell again.

I sectioned off a portion of dough and dropped it in front of him. "Knead it."

He watched me knead the dough and mimicked my hands as I rolled it into a ball. But his dough looked oblong.

"Sorry about that," he said.

The words drew my attention to his face, but he was talking to the dough.

"I'm so sorry." He pressed the heel of his palm into the

dough. "I *knead* you to forgive me, okay?" His attention focused on the dough. "Please forgive me."

Normally, I talked to dough, ingredients, and supplies when I baked, but that was me. He didn't bake or cook when we dated.

Was he indirectly talking to me? Was he asking for my forgiveness? My heart hammered as I pretended not to notice his conversation with the dough.

But sarcasm sparked in me. "Love is made of kneading, stretching, cutting, and shaping."

"Sounds painful, doesn't it?" Cindy asked.

"No pain, no gain," Austin replied.

I should have stopped commenting, but my rebellious inner self was unstoppable today. "Love is an extraordinary pastry made of happy flour and sweet ingredients. Too bad some people add too much salt, yeast, and other distasteful things to the mix and ruin everything."

The room grew quiet for a moment. I could almost feel Cindy and Austin holding their breaths.

What was I doing? I shouldn't let the past be the damning ingredient to this day. "Love is a special ingredient the heart savors." I looked at Cindy and then Austin. "Right?"

"Absolutely!" Cindy cheered.

I returned my attention to the lesson. "The next technique is rolling it into a smooth ball." I demonstrated, and he followed with ease. We continued until we filled a baking sheet and covered it with plastic wrap, letting it rest for fifteen minutes.

While waiting, I busied myself with other tasks. Bianca entered, asking for Austin's assistance.

When he stepped out of the kitchen, the room temperature dropped immediately. The sensation was probably in my head. Somehow, he still had a powerful effect on me.

Austin returned to continue learning how to snip the dough to form the ears. He beat an egg to coat the bread and slid the baking sheet into the oven.

For the next three days, I took paid vacation days from my main job to acclimate myself to the daily routine of the bakery. He showed up on those days to help out. On Thursday, I returned to my day job and stopped by No Name after work. Austin showed up thirty minutes after my arrival.

"What are you doing here?" I asked, knowing the bakery would close in three hours.

"I like it here." He shrugged. "It makes me happy to see baked goods."

"Oh yeah?" Bianca smirked as she carried a tray of cookies. "It's always good when the boss loves what his shop sells."

Standing next to me, Rosie elbowed me and whispered, "I think he means you—a lovely pastry." She licked her lips.

Oh my god. I shook my head and laughed.

Donna and Cindy slid me a smile as they opened boxes and put supplies away.

"I don't think so," I whispered to Rosie.

Austin grabbed another tray of pies and followed Bianca to the front.

"Wanna bet?" Rosie wiggled her eyes. "The winner buys dinner."

"No."

"Why not?" Rosie asked. "I heard he was your ex."

Curious, Donna and Cindy huddled around to listen.

"If I were younger, I'd date him," Donna said. "But my Mikey wouldn't like that."

"What happened?" Cindy asked. "Why did the relationship end?"

I didn't want to talk about my personal life with my new coworkers. Austin was the owner—their employer. Whatever happened between us should remain private. I didn't want my negative experience to give an unattractive portrayal of him.

Austin seemed like a dedicated boss who cared for his employees.

"It's the past." I shrugged. "I just want to focus on the future, you know?"

"Understood." Donna patted my back. "That's a great outlook."

Time flew by when I worked at the bakery. My shift ended, and I slid on my coat and waved to Cindy. Rosie and Donna were inside Bianca's office.

I didn't see Austin around. He had probably gone home already.

Wrong.

He was outside waiting for me. "Want to have dinner? It's my treat for the bread lesson."

"There's no need. I'm a part-time employee. So you basically paid me to teach you."

"Yes. But you did a phenomenal job." His smile turned serious. "Have you considered hearing my explanation?"

No more dodging. I had to face this.

"I have."

"And?" His eyes bore into me.

"Yes, I want to hear what you have to say."

His eyes beamed. "Wanna go now? We can talk over dinner."

"No. I'll let you know when I'm ready."

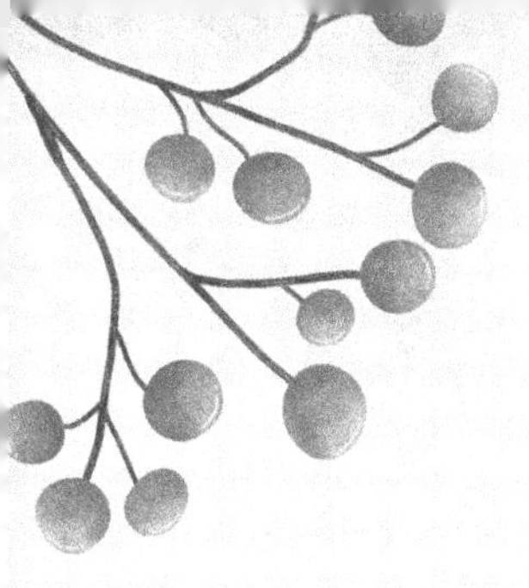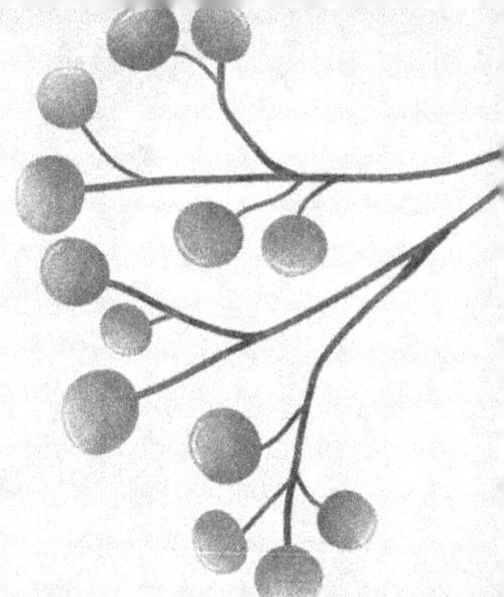

CHAPTER EIGHT

AUSTIN

GETTING to see Ava was the highlight of my day, and I wanted to see her as much as I could. Friday was usually less chaotic, but I had three meetings today because of several new projects. I had my secretary, Louise, shift my schedule around so all the meetings were stacked together. I needed to free up the late afternoon to be at No Name.

If someone had told me two years ago that I'd rearrange my work schedule so I could work at a bakery, I'd have called them a liar. But right now, that was the glaring truth. Being in Ava's presence revitalized my soul in ways I couldn't even imagine. Her smile, her voice, the way her long hair draped around her face, the scent of her floral perfume—everything about her boosted my heart.

I'd dwelled in the dark after our breakup, and seeing her again was the light I desperately needed.

What could be better than seeing her live her dream at the bakery? She'd shared it with me, and I'd cherish that moment till the day I die.

I wasn't a baker, but I'd learned to appreciate the art of baking because of her. During our time together, I'd eaten many of her breads and pastries. I was the lucky man to have tasted her first creations. The excitement and pride on her face the first time she made the bunny-shaped breads still etched in my mind. She'd called the cute bread her bunny buns.

Yesterday, I got the chance to make the adorable bunny bread. The experience swelled my heart like yeast. Or rather, it confirmed something that flared through my body— I *wanted* her back. This was my chance to make things right —my opportunity to tell her I love her.

Would she give me that opportunity? Or was this wishful thinking?

Renewed with hope, I shoved all doubts aside and focused on today's schedule. I had one more meeting before I could leave the office. Tanner Properties just bought five new properties around Worcester County. Worcester was a beautiful city that was becoming a mini Boston, but not as crowded or as expensive yet. The cost of living would climb though.

A retail plaza was in the early stages of development, and an apartment building was slated just one block down, making it convenient for the future residents.

My dad retired after I took over the company. He'd become more mellow and enjoyed traveling with my mom. He and Mom had just come back from their Milan trip. But things weren't this joyful over a year ago. My stomach twisted thinking about the past.

A knock sounded on my door, and I glanced up to see my dad in his brown felt coat. Rising, I walked around my desk and over to greet him. His Parkinson's required him to walk with a cane, which he viewed as a flaw. But time and a new perspective in life had allowed him to accept the progress of life.

"Where's Mom?" I asked, making sure he got to the chair safely. Once settled, I sat across from him on the couch.

"She's chatting with Louise."

Louise and my mom had been friends for a long time. She started out as my dad's secretary when he first opened Tanner Properties.

"Do you want anything to drink?" I asked.

"No, thank you. Your mom and I are meeting up with friends later. Retirement has been a dream." His blue eyes flashed with pride. "Thanks to you."

"You worked hard to start this company. I won't let it fail. It's our family's legacy."

As their only son, the pressure to succeed weighed heavily on me, but I never complained because I enjoyed the work.

"It is." He sighed. "I made many mistakes along the way. I thought I'd made smart decisions but ended up tossing the company into extreme financial peril." Regret strained his face. "I'm sorry for placing you in that difficult position." He leaned back into the couch, looking at me. "Your mom never stops scolding me, you know. I made you lose the love of your life."

What could I say? I didn't want my dad to hold guilt in his heart. The man had recovered from heart surgery and was doing well.

Though resentment lingered in me, I blamed myself for not handling the situation better back then.

"It's not your fault. I didn't tell Ava the truth, and I was reckless in how I ended it."

How could I marry someone I didn't love? The Montages weren't known for their kindness or understanding. I wanted Ava as far away from me—from *them*—as possible.

In my fantasy world, I thought I could get Ava back after things settled. What a fool I was. Why would she want me back after I'd dumped her over text? She didn't want to talk to me and left all my belongings in the box outside of her apartment. Rhea had called me to pick it up. Ava didn't even want any of her belongings that she kept at my place.

"Can you reconcile with Ava?"

"Maybe." *I hope so.*

The reply surprised me. If he had asked me this a month ago, the answer would've been a hard no. But now, I felt hope floating around me.

When my dad asked for this meeting, I wasn't sure what it was about. But now I knew he was seeking forgiveness.

"You made some bad investments, and you were sick and weren't seeing things properly," I said. "But now you're better."

He nodded. "I'm sorry for the pressure I placed on you. The company was failing, and we lost a lot of money. I thought the engagement to the Montage family would help." He placed a hand on his chest. "I want you to be happy, Austin. Don't sacrifice your happiness for the family anymore."

Ava's face appeared in my vision.

"If I hadn't been so stubborn, things would've been easier on you." He glanced up at the ceiling. "Our ancestors are always watching over us. They guided you to a supportive friend to help in times of need." He was referring to Remington Starke, who had invested in me during that difficult time.

I'd met him years ago, and we'd become friends. His financial support helped Tanner Properties from sinking into the black hole. Before I met him, I'd bought an abandoned building close to the thriving business section of Natick. Lack of finances had slowed down my condominium project until Remington. Remi's architect friend, Grayson Wu, helped escalate the exterior and interior design efficiently. It didn't take me long to pay Remi back.

"Your condo project saved our family." My dad grinned. "Why didn't you tell me and your mom about it?"

"It wasn't complete yet, and I didn't want to jinx it, you know?"

"I do." He smiled. "Unlike me, you're thorough and patient."

He rose and walked over to my chair, placing a hand on my shoulder. "Can you forgive me, son?" His eyes gleamed with tears.

I didn't know I needed his apology until it landed in my chest, melting the iceberg that sat at the pit of my stomach.

"Yes." I got up and offered him a hug.

A heavy weight lifted off me, making me feel hopeful. After a quick chat with my mom, my parents headed out to the art museum.

I grabbed my coat and walked out to my car.

"Austin!" Sierra's voice sliced through the air.

I turned to see her rushing up to me with her high-heeled boots. "Where are you going? I have tickets to *A Midsummer*

Night's Dream at the Hanover tomorrow night. I want you to come with me."

It wasn't a question, but a demand.

"I'm busy."

"Doing what?" she retorted.

"I'm seeing someone, *remember?*" I said, reminding her that if any harm were done to me, my family, or my girlfriends after the broken engagement I would release video evidence of her hiring someone to eliminate the daughter of Senator Lawson from New York.

Remi introduced me to some of his friends who could access private information quickly and discreetly. I had to protect myself from the Montages, and now I had plenty of protection.

"So?" She smirked and ran a hand down my arm. "You can still accompany me as a friend."

"She won't like that."

"Why are you hooked on her? Why can't you give us a chance?"

"She respects herself." I stepped back so her hand fell from my arm. "You should too. When someone tells you they're not interested, respect their decision, Sierra. Move on."

She flared her nostrils and glared at me. I imagined darts flying out of her eyes, trying to kill me.

"You're a smart businessman, but you're making an unwise choice, Austin."

"You're a smart woman. Don't make an unwise decision that will take down your precious family. Do I need to show you that video again? I have more recordings that implicate your father. Do you want me to give him a call?"

"You're an ass!" She pouted and stalked back to her Mercedes.

Shaking that irritation off, I drove to No Name, hoping to bake more bunny buns today. But when I got there, Cindy told me Ava wasn't working today.

Though sadness stabbed me, I stayed at the bakery helping to display all of her animal breads. I saved some cute cats and cows to bring home later.

CHAPTER NINE

AVA

FRIDAY DRAGGED on at the office as I wondered how the bakery was doing today. I'd prepared several baking sheets of bunny-, cat-, and cow-shaped breads for them. I couldn't wait to get everyone's feedback. I wished I was at No Name today.

I blinked at the desire. How could it have lured me in so fast? I missed working with Bianca, Donna, Cindy, and Rosie so much.

Who else do you miss?

It was no use lying to myself. I blew out a breath and admitted I missed Austin too. What was wrong with me? Why was I pining after an ex? Obviously, I had unresolved emotions that needed to be dealt with now.

After the despair I'd gone through, I was still attracted to him. The proof was in how my body reacted to his presence. Last night, I had the wildest dream about him. We were both in the kitchen doing all kinds of delicious things to each other.

Saturday arrived, and enthusiasm rushed through me as I got to the bakery. Disappointment stirred in me when noon arrived and Austin was nowhere in sight. Where was he? I'd gotten used to seeing him.

When my shift ended, sadness churned in me.

"Looks like there's an ice storm coming tonight." Bianca glanced at her phone.

"That's what the meteorologist said last week and nothing happened." Cindy zipped up her coat. "Hopefully, they'll be wrong this time too."

"We have a neon display that I can access to update messages in case we have to open later." Bianca crossed her fingers. "Let's hope the storm moves up north and misses us."

Cindy and I waved to Rosie and Donna at the front counter.

"I'm heading to the grocery store." Cindy walked to her car. "See you tomorrow, hopefully."

"Have a good evening." I slid into my car, thinking of browsing the nearby shops.

I had heard customers raving about a new bookstore that recently opened up. I was in the mood for a suspenseful romance novel. Ever since my relationship ended with Austin, I'd healed my heart with baking and reading. In books, everyone got their happily ever after.

I used the shopping therapy to clear my head and figure out when I'd want Austin's explanation.

I found parking near Metaphors & Similes, got out, and entered the bookstore. The decor offered warm colors of pink, peach, and purple. A burgundy couch sat against a wall with rotating bookshelves standing nearby. Several cards hung from a wooden chandelier. As I approached, I saw that each card had a metaphor or simile from popular books.

"Welcome!" said a pretty woman with purple hair, wearing a long lilac dress. "I'm Charlene. Let me know if you have any questions."

"Thank you." I walked over to the little gift section displaying jewelry and art from local artists.

A musky scent snuck up my nose, and I sneezed. My heart raced when I saw a man standing across the table, picking up an intricate necklace. I grabbed a heart-shaped cup and held it, pretending to study it. But I took my time examining the man. Indeed, he wasn't the man in the parking lot who I assumed was the thief who had stolen my emerald bracelet. This man standing before me had short dark hair and wore a leather coat and light jeans. My heart raced as I remembered him from Artisan Jewelers. He'd been looking at something in the store at the same time as me! Not only that, I recalled seeing him at the candle store too. Had he been following me in the mall?

I needed to call Officer Jensen. My hands trembled even though the thief wasn't looking at me. I stepped away, wanting to go outside to call, but bumped into someone. I glanced up and my heart jolted.

"Austin." Without thinking, I grabbed his hand and rushed out the door.

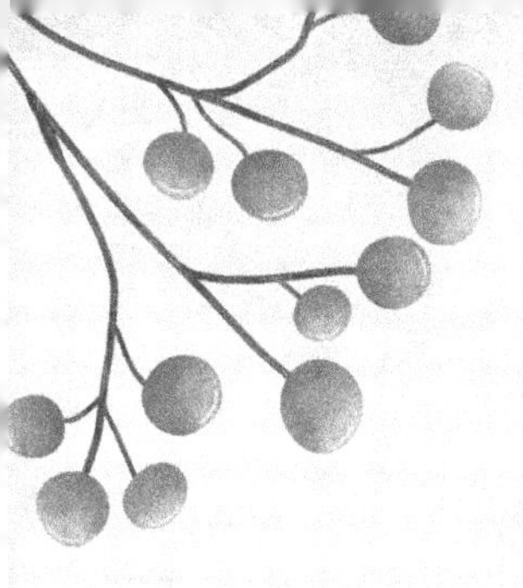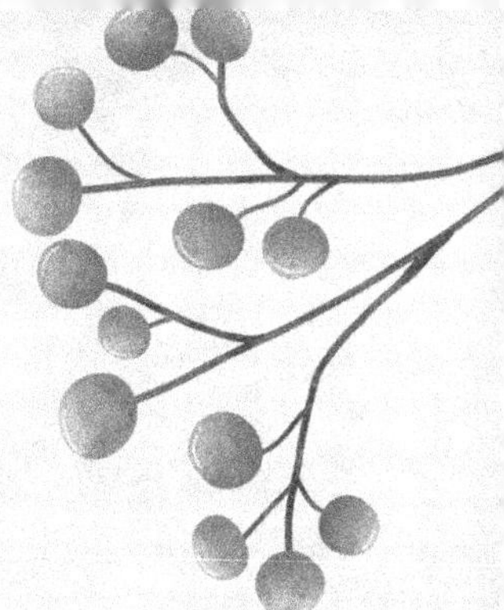

CHAPTER TEN

AUSTIN

I DIDN'T LIKE the fear in her eyes. When we got outside, my hand tightened over hers. "What's wrong?"

"I recognized the man in the bookstore. He's the one who stole my bracelet." Ava extracted her hand from mine to glance in the store window. "He's still there."

"I'll call Jeremy." I took out my phone and alerted him. When I hung up, I took Ava's hand in mine again. "He'll be here soon."

The thief strode out of the bookstore and walked down the street. Ava and I exchanged glances, and a mutual understanding passed between us. We followed him into Annette's Jewelry.

"I've got a plan," I said to Ava.

We entered the jewelry store and walked up to the counter, standing near the man who was being helped by a sales associate with dark hair.

"Hello, my name is Dorothy. Do you need help with anything?" asked a woman with her hair twisted in a bun.

"We have a holiday promotion going on. Twenty-five percent off all gold earrings and rings."

"Thank you," Ava said.

"I'm gifting my fiancée anything she wants today." I lifted her hand and kissed it, loving the feel of her skin on my lips. "What do you want to get, babe?"

She gaped at me. When understanding swam in her eyes, she touched my face with her hand. "You're so sweet, baby. Let me take a look."

Dorothy led Ava to a display case to try on rings while I kept my eyes on the thief.

"How much is this?" Ava asked, admiring a ring on her hand. When Dorothy showed her the price tag, she gasped and laughed. "It's beautiful but that's too much. I don't want my fiancé spending money like that." She tried on another ring, having fun chatting with Dorothy.

Minutes later, the police sirens sounded. The thief glanced up, looking fearful. When he saw the two police cruisers parked across the street, he walked toward the door. I followed him.

As though he sensed something, he swerved to look at me.

"Done stealing?" I asked.

He ran, and I chased after him. When I caught up, a fight ensued. My foot slipped on something, and I fell against a large outdoor pot. My weight shoved it over, shattering the pot. Something sharp slashed my neck.

Shit!

The thief glanced at me, and for a moment, he looked sorry.

"Stop!" Jeremy caught up.

The thief raced forward but was cornered by another officer.

"Oh my gosh!" Ava rushed over to me, helping me up. "Are you okay?"

"I'm fine." I brushed the dirt off my coat as light snow started to fall.

"No, you're not!" She turned my face to the side. "Your neck is bleeding." Concern swam in her eyes.

I ran a hand over the burning sensation, and blood smeared on my fingers. "Just a minor cut. I'll take care of it at home."

Jeremy stopped by with the thief in handcuffs. "I'll be in touch."

"Can I talk to him?" Ava asked.

He looked at Ava and then at me and nodded. "Come this way."

CHAPTER ELEVEN

AVA

AUSTIN and I followed Officer Jensen to his cruiser, where he placed the suspect, named Juan Collazo, in the back seat with the window rolled down. I stepped up and stared at the thief who had despair sagging on his face. His eyes held back tears, while his hunched shoulders and tight jaw illustrated a criminal that perplexed me. Austin took my hand and offered me comfort while narrowing his eyes at Juan.

Officer Jensen stood beside his cruiser, making sure Juan behaved.

"Why do you take things that don't belong to you?" I asked.

From this close proximity, he didn't look like the terrifying criminal that had formed in my head. He closed his eyes for a moment. Releasing a heavy sigh, he opened his eyes and met mine. Regret swam in them.

"I didn't want to," he said.

"That's what all criminals say when they're caught." Austin squeezed my hand.

"I really didn't want to." Juan swallowed, pushing back tears.

What was going on?

"When did you take the bracelet from me?"

"At the candle store. It was crowded there that day. I'm sorry," he said. "My daughter is very sick. She needs surgery, and I don't have the money to pay for it." He paused. "They promised me a portion of what they'd sell on the black market. I'm sorry."

Something shifted inside me.

"Who's 'they'?" Officer Jensen asked.

"People I met through an acquaintance." Juan described them to Officer Jensen. "I cleaned her house a few times."

My stomach twisted in knots as Officer Jensen asked Juan more questions and told him he'd need to repeat everything at the precinct with his lawyer present. When my mom was sick, her health insurance didn't pay for all the treatments. She used her savings for it. I could imagine the stress Juan was going through.

Officer Jensen rolled up the window of his cruiser and turned to us. "Sounds like his acquaintances are part of a New York gang that's been hitting a lot of stores. We have a team investigating this. But I'll confirm once I look into them."

"Can you please keep me updated on this case?" I asked, trying to decipher the meaning of justice.

"Of course." Officer Jensen saluted Austin and slid into his cruiser.

As Austin walked me to my car, I said, "You should let the cops chase after the criminal. What if he had a gun or something?"

He brushed a hand over my face. "I didn't want him to escape. He stole something from you, so he needs to pay."

"Don't be reckless. I can replace the bracelet."

"Worried about me?"

When I didn't reply, he bent down and kissed me. His lips were warm against mine. My heart thundered, and desire scorched through me, jolting my body awake. It had been so long since my body felt this powerful reaction.

"I missed you," he said.

I felt the wounds between us healing quietly, broke the kiss, and breathed. "I'm ready for the explanation."

CHAPTER TWELVE

AVA

I DROVE my car to Austin's house, which was in a recent development on sought-after Salisbury Street. I parked in the spacious lot with three car garages.

"When did you buy this house?" I admired the brick exterior as I walked up the steps. He'd upgraded from his previous one.

"Six months ago." He slid off his coat and hung it in the closet in the marble foyer. "Let me take your coat."

While he hung my coat, my gaze spotted the porcelain vase I'd painted with him. My heart quickened. I'd assumed he'd tossed it after our breakup.

"Do you want a tour?"

"After I clean your cut."

We walked into the spacious bathroom near the kitchen, and he got out a small emergency kit. With a cotton ball, I cleansed his cut, which wasn't big. Then I put some ointment on it and covered it with a bandage.

He looked at his neck. "It's not that bad."

"Better safe than sorry. I don't want you getting an infection."

"Okay." He smiled, rubbing his finger over the bandage.

"How did you know I was in the bookstore?"

"I was heading to the bakery and saw you park. So I stopped, wanting to see you."

"Why?"

"Because seeing you makes me happy."

My heart thundered in my chest.

"Ready for a tour now?"

I followed him to the living room, where comfortable brown couches surrounded a round wooden table. Two chairs were still wrapped in plastic.

"They're still new," I said.

"I'm not sure where to put them yet. There are a few rooms that need to be furnished."

His family room needed a table and some chairs to warm it up. A spacious and empty room could be used as a library or an office. His walls desperately needed art. Though the home was lovely, it needed a few things to make it cozy.

When he led me into his kitchen, my mouth dropped. "Wow." I gawked at his massive kitchen. "Do you cook now?"

"No." He grinned, watching me as I ran my hands over the fine ivory marble counter.

"Then why do you have such an enormous kitchen?"

"For a woman I had in mind." He took my hand in his. "It's for *you*."

The confession made my feet feel like jelly, but I had to be cautious.

He gripped my hand tight as though he feared I'd escape.

I didn't mind him holding my hand. It comforted me more than I realized.

"We weren't together," I muttered, trying to understand why he'd make a kitchen for me.

He kissed my hand again. When he'd done it in the jewelry store, I'd wished it wasn't a pretense.

"You're the only one I want."

Pain and betrayal flooded back into my memory, and I extracted my hand from his grip. "You broke up with me, Austin. You were engaged."

"And I broke off the engagement a month later. It would've been sooner, but my father is a stubborn man to convince."

"Your father? I don't understand."

"Come sit down. It's time for the explanation."

I followed him into the living room and sat on the comfortable couch.

"Do you want anything to drink? I've got tea, hot chocolate, and wine."

The wine would probably help settle my nerves, but tea was better for me. "Tea, please."

"Got it." He took the remote and pressed a button. The horizontal electric fireplace lit up, casting a warm glow on the wall and in the room.

He brought back a glass of wine for himself and a cup of tea for me.

"I should've handled the situation better." He sat beside me and sighed, looking nervous. "I never wanted to be engaged to Sierra. I've never dated her."

I remembered seeing all her social media posts declaring she was engaged to Austin Tanner of Tanner Properties. The news had hit me like a slab of ice, knocking me down for weeks.

My eyebrows furrowed. "So the engagement just appeared out of the blue?"

"Sort of." He sipped and placed the wine glass on the table. "Tanner Properties was suffering a major financial loss. My father's health was going downhill. He thought marrying a Montage would keep the company alive. Marcus Montage told my dad his daughter liked me."

I couldn't believe what I was hearing. I finished my tea as I listened to the arranged engagement, how he'd ended it, and how Sierra continued to pursue him. Austin also shared about his father's heart surgery, a stroke that nearly left him paralyzed, and Parkinson's disease. My body tensed as though I felt the pressure he'd been under. Austin explained how his condo investment had helped Tanner Properties bounce back without the help of the Montage family. Austin led the company out of the dark all by himself.

"I was an ass for sending you the text." He grabbed my hand with both of his. "I have so much I want to say. I'm so sorry for the pain I caused." He looked at me and pain and regret stirred in them. "I couldn't bear the thought of seeing you . . . Saying those things to you would've been like knifing myself with each word. I couldn't do it. Hearing your voice on the phone would've been the same as seeing you. I love you. That has never changed and will never change, Ava."

My heart trembled. "Why didn't you tell me all this afterwards?"

"You didn't want to talk to me, remember?"

I recalled the anger that had cut into me. The betrayal was like salt dumped onto a raw wound. At that time, nothing he said would've made me feel better. My heart had been ripped wide open, and I was too angry and hurt. I needed to protect myself. Seeing him and talking to him would have only reminded me of the pain he'd caused.

"Yeah," I said, wishing the situation had been different. I wished I could have forgiven him enough to listen to his explanation.

"There's a reason for everything," he said. "That time away from each other allowed me to grow. My love for you grew even though you weren't with me. It sounds weird, doesn't it?"

A clump formed in my throat as tears slid down my face. "No, it makes sense. I couldn't let you go either. I thought of you all the time and cursed myself for it."

He grabbed a tissue from the box on the side table and dabbed my eyes. "I guess the statement is true: distance makes the heart grow fonder."

Because tears wouldn't stop, he offered the entire box of tissues. "Thanks. I wanted to give up on my dream so many times."

"To have your own bakery?"

I nodded. "You were the only person I shared it with. I associated that dream with *you*—the man I love."

"Ava." He pulled me into his arms, kissing the top of my head. I felt his heart thumping wildly. "Never let go of your dreams for *anyone*. Not even for me." He dropped another kiss on my forehead. "You have no idea how much I love you."

His words soothed the pressure in my chest.

"My savings dwindled. I thought it was a sign that my dream was dwindling too, that it was just an illusion tricking me into believing in it. The more the savings disappeared, the more I felt hopeless about my dream."

I told him about the car repairs, the burst pipe, my mom's bracelet, and her recovery from breast cancer.

"I should've been there for you." His arms tightened around me.

"You had a lot going on." I touched his face, rubbing out the crease between his eyebrows.

"Is your mom doing better now?"

"She is. Thank you." I smiled. "Her friends are keeping her busy."

"That's excellent news." Regret strained his face. "We've let so much time pass, Ava."

"We both had a rough year." I traced his square jaw with my finger. "But you're right—everything we've been through made us better." I kissed his chin. "It's like baking bread. Every pat, every squeeze, and every knead makes the dough stronger so it can rise to become what it needs to be."

"That's a marvelous analogy." Amusement gleamed in his eyes. "Only you could see meaning in something like that. I love it." He kissed me, and his warm lips chased away all the doubts that had clung to me. "I missed you so much."

"I missed you too." I kissed him back.

The dam that had contained my emotions broke free. I needed to feel all the feelings again. My fingers gripped his hair, wanting him closer. He felt my urgency and responded effectively with tongue and teeth. He growled and sucked my tongue. Our mouths devoured each other as though we'd never see each other again. Heat spread through me, and I moaned, wanting more. He drew back, staring at me with darkened eyes. "I want you in my bed."

I smirked. "Lead the way, handsome."

CHAPTER THIRTEEN

AVA

HE GOT up from the couch and grabbed my hand, yanking me up. I leaped into his arms and wrapped my legs around his waist.

One strong arm supported my back, while the other cupped my ass. "Gorgeous bun." He smiled and kneaded my cheeks. "So perfect."

Austin carried me down a hallway with beautiful hardwood floors. The wall sconces lit up as we passed. He slowed his steps as he dropped kisses along the column of my neck. A moan escaped me, needing to be kissed and touched by this man. Heat rose in my core, spreading all over me. I inhaled his musky cologne, an irresistible scent I'd recognize anywhere. Every part of my body became alive from his scent.

His mouth met mine again, and desire shot through the roof.

I knew we made it to his bed when my back hit soft sheets. He hovered over me, looking down at me with lust in his eyes.

"I've been dreaming about this." He brushed his fingers down my cheek. "You in my home. My bed."

"I had an erotic dream about you," I confessed.

"Really?" A devilish smirk slid onto his face. "Tell me more."

"Strip and I'll share."

Immediately, his shirt and jeans flew onto the floor, making me laugh. I sat up watching him step out of his boxers.

Oh my.

The sight of his glorious cock made my throat dry. My eyes raked his entire body. Deliciously fit and firm. I scooted closer to the edge of the bed and ran a hand over his strong shoulders. I took my time moving down his arm, to the outstanding abdomen that could be used as my cutting board, and his powerful thighs and legs.

"Like what you see?" Austin asked in a husky voice.

"Very much." I slid my hand down to his cock, gripped it, and squeezed. "It's been a while. Miss me?"

It twitched and swelled in my hand. The inner muscles of my thighs flexed, remembering what his cock could do to me.

Austin nudged me back onto the bed. "My turn." He removed my sweater, bra, pants, and panties. Growling, he claimed a breast with his eager mouth.

Pleasure exploded in me as my hands flew to his head, holding it in place. It had been so long since I was loved like this.

I arched my back. "More."

He grinned and feasted on the other breast. My legs wrapped around him, loving the feel of his hot cock against my skin.

I roamed my hands over his back and squeezed his firm ass. "My beautiful buns."

He lifted his head, and amusement flickered in those blue eyes. "My buns are yours as your buns are mine."

I laughed, loving the playfulness. A wolfish grin flashed on his lips as he spread my thighs. With an open mouth, he skimmed along my inner thigh, igniting a trail of fire. My thighs trembled from the increasing energy blooming in my core.

When his mouth pressed into me, I cried. "Oh my God!"

The onslaught of sensations pushed my thighs in, but he held them in place. "I've been hungry for you."

His skillful tongue was like a magical whisk that churned me through and through. My entire body softened as need pushed and pulled, thrashing me from side to side. I shivered when liquid heat leaked out of me.

"That's it, love." He crooned as he licked me again and again. "You taste so good."

Pressure increased between my thighs. When he shoved two fingers into me and sucked my bud, I climaxed.

"Austin!" Bliss burst through me, sending a surge of energy shooting to the top of my head.

"God, I love seeing you come undone." He rose and positioned himself between my legs.

I was still gasping for breath when he slid into me.

"So tight," he moaned and met my eyes. "You okay?"

"Never been better."

With that statement, he pummeled into me, hard and fast. Our moans and blissful cries filled his bedroom. He kept going until his body tensed. I watched his face as the orgasm erupted within him. Heat filled me as his body shook from the massive quake.

"So good," he said and thrust into me once more.

Then he dropped onto my body, bracing a hand on the side so he wouldn't crush me. With his cock still inside me, he dropped a kiss onto my forehead. "Sorry, I forgot the condom. I'm clean. I haven't been with anyone since you."

"Really?"

He nodded, and his cock twitched inside me. "Only you can turn me on."

I smiled as he rolled off me and ran to the bathroom. I glanced around his spacious bedroom. It had a nightstand and a large bureau on the other side of the wall. A tall lamp stood in the corner. Brown curtains covered the window. The ambiance of the bedroom could improve with a chair, another lamp, some artwork, maybe a candle, and plants.

He returned with a towel to clean me. He'd always done this, and I loved watching him care for me.

"What are you thinking?" He dropped the towel to the floor and slid back into bed with me.

I curled up against him. "Admiring and decorating your bedroom in my head."

"I was hoping you would." He pulled me closer. "I haven't done much to it."

His phone rang, and he reached for his jeans, pulling out his phone.

"Hey, Jeremy. What's up?" Austin listened, nodded, and said, "I'm putting you on speaker so Ava can hear too."

"Hi Ava," said Officer Jensen. After I returned his greeting, he said, "I've got an update for you."

"Did you catch his accomplices?"

"Will soon. Juan is going to help us." Officer Jensen sighed. "He doesn't have a record. I spoke to his boss at a cleaning company. He's hardworking and doesn't create conflicts. Apparently, Juan's twelve-year-old daughter has a brain tumor, and insurance isn't paying a lot. These men promised to give him a portion of the sales of the stolen goods. So far, he has received none. He felt bad about stealing but didn't know how else to help his daughter."

A brain tumor.

"What's going to happen to him?" I asked.

"If we catch the other suspects and recover all the stolen items, it'll help his case."

I didn't know if I was doing the right thing, but my heart told me to help Juan.

"He didn't steal out of greed or malice. He stole out of a need for his daughter. I don't want him to go to jail for that." I tried to imagine the fear and worry that probably gripped him. "Maybe he can do community service or something? His family needs him around."

To me, it wasn't justice to send Juan to prison because he wanted to save his family.

Austin rubbed a hand on my back. "Is that something you can do, Jeremy?"

"I'll try my best. I'll speak to the prosecutor to see what he can do. We want the shark. Juan was a small, desperate fish that swam and trusted the wrong people."

"What if I don't want to press charges for my bracelet?" I asked, meeting Austin's curious eyes.

"That would help him too."

While Austin chatted with Officer Jensen about holiday plans, I thought about all the families who were worried about a loved one. I was grateful my mom's chemotherapy went well. But I remembered the anxiety that kept me up at night. I didn't know Juan, but I believed we all deserve a second chance.

I looked at Austin, who was still on the phone. We got our second chance. I reached for my clothes, got dressed, walked over to the window, and pushed the curtains aside to see a sheet of ice on the back patio. *Ugh.* It was going to be a pain removing the ice from my car. I had to head home, shower, and sleep to prepare for tomorrow.

"Where are you going?" Austin wrapped his hands around my waist, nuzzling my neck.

"Home."

"It's too dangerous. Didn't you hear Jeremy say only essential people are allowed in the street for the next twenty-four to forty-eight hours? The ice storm is worse than they expected."

"What?" Anxiety bubbled in my stomach. "Let me see my car."

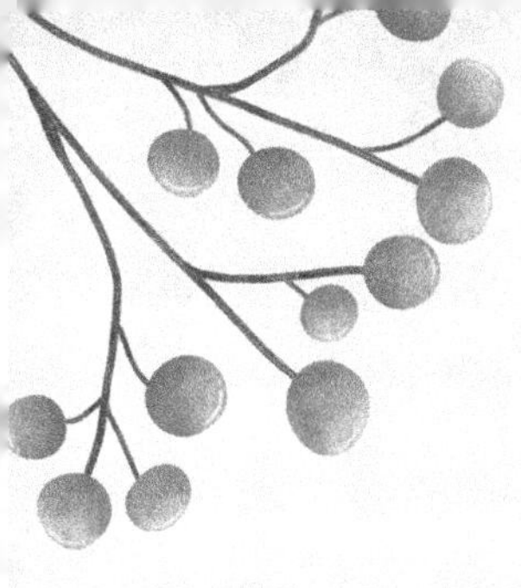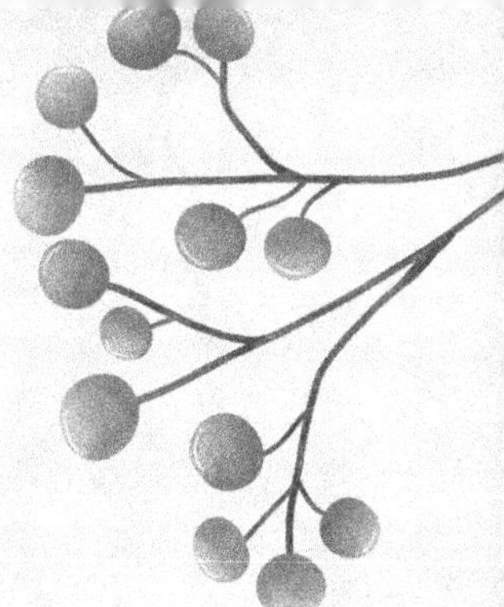

CHAPTER FOURTEEN

AUSTIN

SLEET SLAPPED against the window as Ava looked outside at the driveway.

"You're stuck with me." I led her back to the couch.

We turned on the TV and watched the news reporters relay the city's message about staying home. Though the city had treated the roads, the sleet and the quick drop in temperature made traveling dangerous. Ice wasn't like snow, where the snowplows could remove it easily.

"The bakery will have to close?" she asked, still looking anxious.

"Yes, I'll notify Bianca now." I sent her a text and placed my phone on the coffee table. "Are you okay? You don't want to stay here with me?"

"We're just starting over, and I don't want to intrude."

"You're definitely not intruding." I leaned into her. "You're making my dream come true. We used to take turns staying at each other's homes, remember?"

She nodded, and her stomach growled.

"What do you want for dinner?" I smiled. "I've got leftovers."

"I need a shower first, but I don't have any clothes."

"Yes, you do."

"I do?"

Rising, I led her to the guest room on the first floor and gestured to the closet and drawers. "Look."

With furrowed eyebrows, she ambled over to the closet and saw the jackets and coats she'd left at my old place. She opened a drawer and sucked in a breath. "You kept all my clothes?"

"Everything."

"Even the toiletries?" Her eyes widened.

I nodded. "But check the expiration date on the creams and lotions."

She pulled out a set of pink cotton pajamas and a pair of panties. "Where's the shower?"

"Want me to join you?"

"Okay." Wickedness sparked in her eyes.

I enjoyed the unforgettable shower where she screamed out my name so many times. I loved the sound of her blissful cries and how her body went lax after the orgasm.

After the steamy shower, we got dressed and returned to the kitchen.

"I'm not that hungry anymore." She popped green grapes into her mouth as she sat on the stool, looking satisfied and cozy in her pajamas.

She picked out a gray top and striped bottoms for me, the set she'd gotten me when we first started dating.

"But you will be soon." I took the warm fried rice out of the microwave and placed it on the counter. I got out plates and checked the oven. Ten more minutes before the frozen pizza would be ready.

I brought over a pastry box and set it in front of her. "Want some?"

She opened the box and tilted her head up, looking delighted. "When did you get these?"

"The day you were off. I helped Cindy bake them. They're cute." I picked up the cat bun and bit into it. "So good. You can make an entire animal series."

"Plan to."

She watched me finish her cat bun, and a question flickered in those brown eyes.

"What is it?"

"Why is the bakery called No Name?"

"Because I wanted you to name it."

"What?" Emotions stormed her eyes.

"I opened the bakery for you," I admitted.

"But . . . but we weren't together then."

"It didn't matter." I shrugged. "Opening the bakery made me feel closer to you. Though I didn't know anything about baking or running a bakery, I made it happen. Did my research, hired the right people, and invested in a dream that was important to me."

Ava shifted, threw her arms around me, and cried. "I love you."

"I love you too." I inhaled her hair, which had the scent of my shampoo. "What do you want to call it?"

She drew back and considered. "Not sure yet. So, I can name it anything?"

"Anything. The bakery is yours."

She blinked. "What do you mean?"

"We own it together. I put you down as part owner when I started it."

"Austin, that's risky!" she huffed. "How could you be sure we'd get back together? What if—"

"My mission was to get you back no matter what it takes. When I saw Bianca had hired you as the part-time baker, I knew that was a sign. Christmas came early for me."

"I don't know what to say."

"Say you'll help me make it the most successful bakery in the city."

Tears welled up in her eyes. "I'll try my best."

I tipped up her chin, thumbed away her tears, kissed her, and asked a question that would make her smile. "You never told me about the dream." I wiggled my eyebrows. "Was I hot in it? What was I wearing?"

As expected, her lips curved. "You were scorching hot." She pressed a finger to my chest and made a sizzling sound. Her eyes slid down to my pants. "You were giving me baking lessons in the nude."

With a laugh, I tried to imagine that. "Oh yeah?"

She palmed the obvious bulge in my pants. "You said he was a skilled mixer that could churn me into a pile of sexy mush." Her eyes gleamed with mischief. "It's cheesy, but it made the dream extra special."

Another roar of laughter escaped me, echoing in my kitchen. An image popped into my vision, and I couldn't dismiss it. The oven beeped, signifying the pizza was finished. I took it out and set it on the wooden block. I wasn't in the mood for pizza or rice right now.

I rushed back, stood behind her, and slipped my arms around her, cupping her breasts. "How's my *kneading*?" I dropped kisses on her neck.

She leaned back into me, letting me play with her gorgeous breasts.

"At this rate. We'll never have dinner," she moaned.

"That's okay. We're making up for lost time." I slipped my hands under her top, rolling her nipples between my fingers. "Dinner can wait. I've got baking lessons to give."

"I can't wait." She laughed and lifted her arms for me to remove her knit top.

I'd never had a naked woman in my kitchen until now. "So what else happened in your dream? I'm going to make it a reality."

She smiled. "You showed me all the ways we could whip up pleasure in the kitchen."

In seconds, my clothes flew to the floor. She got off the stool so I could strip off the rest of her clothes, and I turned her around to face the kitchen island.

She bent over as I spread her legs and found her wet. "All ready for me, baby?"

She moaned into my hands. "You're good at this . . ."

"This what?" I asked, shoving a finger into her.

"Baking . . ." She arched her back with her gorgeous ass beckoning me.

Unable to resist, I dropped to my knees and squeezed her firm buttocks. Her liquid heat glistened, and I licked it.

"Austin!"

God, I'd missed her taste.

"Can't let this juice go to waste." I feasted on her and earned a magnificent orgasm.

We spent the next hour fucking near the stove and the refrigerator. Then she nudged me against the marble island and got on her knees.

"What's going on?" I asked, looking down at my love.

"Such an enticing cannolo." Ava gripped my cock in her grip, stroking seductively.

A laugh bubbled out of me. This was the first time Ava had referred to my cock as a cannolo. Distance had brought us closer, adding humor, amusement, and depth to our relationship.

I loved the look of her all naked on my kitchen floor, pleasuring me with her hand. When she bent down and kissed me, I sucked in a breath, unable to take my eyes away from her. Those luscious lips and tongue sliding down my length while meeting my gaze.

"This is our version of beautiful 'baking.'" She smirked like a vixen knowing exactly what she was doing.

When she took me into her mouth, I crooned and braced a hand on the kitchen island for stability. My fingers curled into her hair, watching her eat me like a wild woman.

For the next thirty minutes, she redefined the definition of a cannolo. I'd never look at it in the same way, and I vowed to make sure we had "beautiful baking" on our home menu from now on.

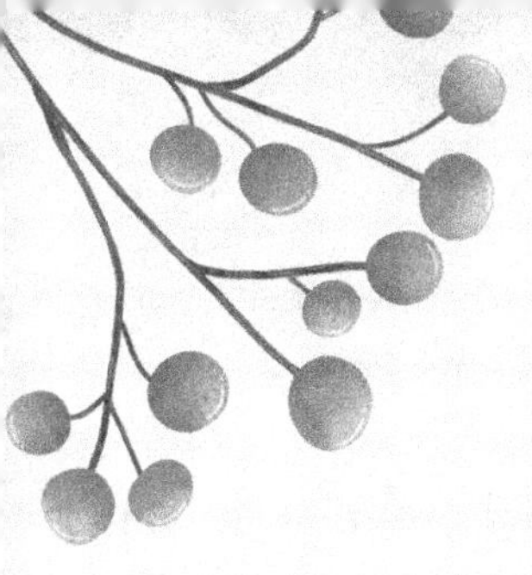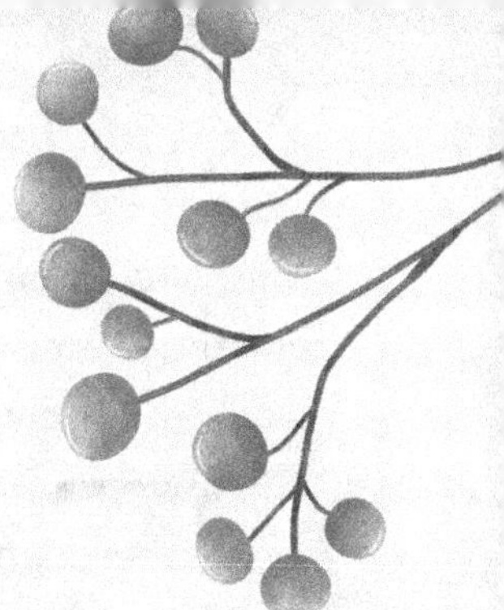

CHAPTER FIFTEEN

AUSTIN

A FEW DAYS LATER, I took the day off from work to tackle an important baking mission.

With hands on my hips and a brand-new apron, I stared at the chaos in my kitchen, which had been spotless until today. I hardly used it because ordering in was easier for a single guy like me. But now flour, sugar, yeast, measuring cups, a mixer, a whisk, a rolling pin, and tin molds were scattered all over the marble counter.

What the hell was I doing? I didn't cook or bake, but I'd do anything to win Ava's heart. I wanted her to know that I loved her without a doubt.

I followed the recipes from No Name that Bianca gave me. With help from some online baking videos, things progressed slowly but surely. After preparing several loaves of bread, pastry buns, and muffins, I was exhausted.

I took a bathroom break and gasped when I saw myself in the mirror. Flour covered my hair in uneven sections, like a bad hair dye. Batter and butter smeared on my face, and a glob of egg custard clung to the side of my nose and chin.

Shit. My apron looked worse. After cleaning my face, I got out the brand-new baking sheets. The floured hair had to wait until I showered.

Two hours later, I stared at the magnificent miracles on my marble counter: a loaf of bread in the shape of a cat, a loaf that sort of looked like a bunny, another loaf that could pass for a bear, a dozen blueberry muffins, animal-shaped buns, apple tarts, and a heart-shaped pumpkin bread. Satisfied, I took out a pack of small notecards and wrote phrases for Ava.

When the baked goods had cooled, I placed them on a large decorative tray along with the notecards. I smiled as I placed the last card between two cat-shaped buns filled with egg custard. It read, *"You knead me, and I knead you."*

I took an egg-custard bun and bit into it and spat it out. "Gross!"

I'd probably mixed up the sugar and salt or misread the directions. Hey, I was a newbie who did all this by myself without burning the house down. That deserved recognition in my opinion.

Sighing, I made a new notecard that read, *"DO NOT EAT. For Display Only!"* and placed it in the center of the tray so everyone could see it.

CHAPTER SIXTEEN

AVA

ON THURSDAY, I stopped by my mom's place before heading to the bakery.

"Do you want to take some with you?" She stirred the pot of chicken noodle soup.

"I'll never say no to your chicken soup." I smiled, taking a seat at the kitchen table. I placed my purse on the chair beside me, watching my mom scoop soup into a container.

Her light brown hair with silver mixed in had grown past her chin now. "I like your bob cut. Looks elegant."

"I think so too." She turned, patted her hair, and smiled, looking healthy like a polished gem.

She used to have mid-length hair that she always wore in a ponytail.

"Things are going well with you and Austin?" Mom placed the bag containing the soup on the table and sat across from me.

"Yes, we're taking it slowly." I explained the story of why he had to end things and how his father was old-fashioned with certain beliefs.

"What? Who still believes in arranged marriages these days? What a stubborn man!" She huffed out a breath. "Everyone knows about the Montage family. You don't do business with them. Period. They're vindictive. I heard of a wife who hired someone to crash into her husband's mistress's car because she knew he was still seeing her even though he told her they had broken up."

I missed that news. "The wife wanted the mistress dead?"

"They'd do anything to crush their enemies." Mom sighed.

"Is the mistress okay?"

"She got some bruises and a broken leg, but she walked away with money after she sued them. The Montages paid off people to keep it out of the news, but I heard from a friend who knew the mistress personally."

"Crazy rich people."

"I understand now." Mom sighed and reached across the table for my hand. "Austin wanted them to know it was over between you and him while he tried to convince his father, who was in a vulnerable condition."

Austin had to be gentle in his request and delivery, which was why it took him a month to break off the engagement.

"Did he break it off via text?" Mom asked sarcastically.

I laughed. "No. He and his father sat down with Sierra and her father."

Pushing the past aside, I looked at my beautiful mother. "I've got something for you." I reached into my purse and pulled out the velvet box. "It's an early Christmas gift."

"Oh sweetie, you could've waited until Christmas." She

held the jewelry box, examining it. "Do you want yours now too?"

"No, mine can wait." I gestured to the box. "Open it."

I watched as her face transformed.

"Oh my gosh! Ava!" Her eyes brightened with tears. "I *love* it. This is the bracelet from the commercial!" She got up and embraced me. "Help me put it on."

I didn't tell her I was among the several people who had been robbed recently. It would only have worried her.

"I'm showing this off tonight when I go out with the girls for dinner. Thank you, sweetie."

Seeing the joy on my mother's face added a layer of peace to my heart.

CHAPTER SEVENTEEN

AVA

THE REST of the week flew by, and Saturday arrived with me starting at No Name early in the morning. Austin had to help his parents with a new furniture delivery, so he'd be coming to the bakery later today.

We were dating again. It had only been a week since that icy storm, but our relationship had gotten steamier each day.

I spent most of the previous week at his house and loved every minute. Austin had asked me to move in with him, but I declined because it was too soon.

Though we had resumed our relationship, I needed to protect myself. I still remembered the heartache and didn't want to ever experience that again, so I wanted to take my time.

I spoke to my mother the day before and told her about Austin and me. Though she was happy for me, she asked me to be careful. I understood her concern. She was my mother, who had seen me at my worst, so she was being protective.

Officer Jensen called me last night to let me know Juan had successfully lured out the members of a New York gang responsible for the thefts around the nation. The WPD was now working with other law-enforcement agencies nation-wide to apprehend the rest of the crew. I learned Juan was doing community service at a homeless shelter as part of his plea bargain.

"Do you know Sierra Montage?" Officer Jensen had asked.

My stomach contorted. "Not personally. Why?"

"She was Juan's acquaintance. He met Sierra when he cleaned her house. She hired him to hurt you, but he couldn't do it, so he took the bracelet instead."

My jaw dropped. "She's crazy."

"Not going to disagree with you. She's also linked to the New York gang. We're working that angle now."

"Oh my god," I said, wondering if those gang members would have followed through with the plan to hurt me.

"The DA is building a case against the Montage family. This new evidence will help him immensely. As far as I know, you're not in danger anymore. Sierra has new targets."

Officer Jensen showed me pictures of three men who were at the mall that day. Two of them were the men who stole my parking spot. The third was the man who had yanked at my purse. A chill rushed down my body, remembering how close I'd been to those dangerous men. I prayed Sierra and her family would get the punishment they deserve.

During my lunch break, I used my tablet and had a conference call with my friends, who

all had various backgrounds and cultures. My Scottish background seemed mundane compared to all the stories they shared with me. I loved these girls like sisters, and it was time they knew about me and Austin.

"I can't wait for the holiday gathering next week!" I waved, missing my friends.

"I've got beauty samples for you guys." Kendra, my Vietnamese-American friend, showed off a bag in front of the camera.

"I need a good moisturizer for my dry skin." Rhea patted her adorable face, which was sprinkled with freckles.

"I'm looking for deep conditioner for my hair." Layla secured a sparkling clip to her black hair.

"So what's going on, Ava?" Jemma asked as she adjusted the side braid with showed off the highlights in her brown hair. "You seem happier."

"You're right." Deidre pursed her lips, studying me with green eyes that made her look like a Greek Goddess. "Come closer to the screen."

I laughed. "So you can see my blackheads?"

"Are you seeing someone?" Kendra asked.

"Yes, that's why I called this meeting." I took a deep breath and told them everything.

"Wow." Kendra shook her head. "That's some story."

"We forgive him then," Jemma said.

"I'm so happy for you!" Rhea exclaimed, followed by Deidre and Layla.

I chatted with them for a few more minutes before logging off and getting back to work.

As I kneaded dough in the kitchen, I felt a lightness in my heart as though it had grown wings ready to soar.

The more time I spent at No Name, the more I wanted to resign from my city job. This place made my heart soar. This bakery was my dream, and my boyfriend helped make it happen.

"What's that smile about?" Cindy asked as she placed the raspberry Danishes onto the tray.

"Nothing."

Cindy snorted. "You can't lie."

I grinned. "Things are going smoothly. I'm just appreciating the moments."

"Is that all?" She wiggled her eyebrows. "You and our handsome boss make the perfect item. How come you didn't want to tell us about your past with him?"

"Sometimes the past makes me sad, and I didn't want to make you sad too. We're together again, so that's all that matters."

"I understand." Her eyes warmed. "He loves you. We all see it."

I *felt* it. But it was nice to hear that others witnessed it too.

"She's such a bitch!" Rosie huffed as she stalked in. "I wish Bianca were here."

Bianca had taken the day off for her twins' birthday celebration.

"Who?" Cindy and I asked simultaneously.

Rosie scrunched up her face in disgust. "I can't believe Austin was engaged to the witch. What an entitled brat! She's out there making snide remarks about our gorgeous pastries."

Pissed, I wiped my hands and strode out to the front with Cindy right behind me. My conversation with Officer Jensen flashed into my head.

Sierra looked exactly like the images from the internet. Straight blonde hair and wearing a belted wool coat over long, sleek boots. Her makeup was perfectly done, and she carried a purse with the Versace logo glinting against the lights. She stood with a woman with curly hair, in a red coat over skinny jeans. She wore a furry crossover purse that made me cringe.

"Who would eat those bunny breads?" Sierra pointed. "They look ugly. Don't you think so, Becca?"

"Disgusting." Becca made a disapproving sound and waved her hand. "I'm surprised this bakery is still in business. Who's the untalented baker?"

An old woman who was looking at the brownies turned around and said, "I know many people who love these adorable bunny breads. I'm one of them. You should try to be nice. It'll make you both prettier."

Sierra rolled her eyes at the woman. "They're atrocious!"

At that moment, Kendra strode in, smiled at me, glanced at Sierra, and knew I needed a minute. She walked over to Donna, who was packing up baked goods in a box.

"If you don't like our pastries, then leave," I said. "We don't want disrespectful people in our shop. They're like mold, ruining everything."

"How dare you speak to me like that?" Sierra surveyed me. "You're the one who ruined my engagement. I can't believe Austin broke it off with me for you."

"I had nothing to do with you throwing yourself at my man." I walked over to the bread counter, protective of my adorable creations. "He was smart enough to know a spoiled brat isn't good for him. Mold is poisonous." I smiled.

"How dare you speak to us that way?" Sierra huffed. "You're just *bakers*. Do you know who we are?"

Cindy laughed. "Yeah—*vulgar and malicious hellions!* Do you know who *we* are?" She placed a hand on each hip. "We're the best bakers in the city, and we're proud of it."

Sierra and Becca gasped, unable to respond. I smirked at Cindy, whose face was red with anger.

"Any more comments, ladies?" Kendra held up her phone, which had been recording the event since she had entered the shop. "Smile. You're gonna be famous! Since when does the Montage family go into small businesses and insult hardworking people?" She moved her phone to record the animal-shaped breads. "How can you call these adorable bunnies *ugly, disgusting,* and *atrocious?*"

Sierra turned away from Kendra's phone. "Get away from me!" Her phone rang and she dug into her purse? "Hi, Dad. I'm shopping." She flicked us an annoyed glance. "At the police precinct? Why?" Her expression changed from arrogance to fear. Then she stalked out of the bakery with Becca behind her.

A small smile crept onto my lips as I quietly thanked the WPD for working fast.

Kendra added a comment to her video, typed something on her phone, and scoffed. "There. Let the evil witches get what they deserve. The internet will give those Karens some love." She walked up to me. "You okay?"

"Fine. She's a horrible person."

"Horrible is too nice of a word," Cindy huffed.

"I agree. I have better adjectives to describe her," Donna said as she packaged the brownies for the old woman. "Thank you and have a great day."

"This is my favorite bakery in the entire state," said the friendly old woman.

"Thank you." I smiled as Rosie emerged with a large tray of apple tarts.

"I heard everything back there." Rosie grinned. "You guys were amazing!"

"She brought out the bitch in me," Cindy snarled.

"I like this version of you." I patted her back. "Are you all right?"

"There are too many people like them in this world. They're flour on the floor." She waved a hand. "They don't bother me."

Sierra and Becca's disturbance didn't bother me either. I knew Sierra was jealous and wanted to hurt me and Austin. I hoped she'd find peace and move on.

"What are you doing here?" I turned to Kendra. "You just bought a box of pastries two days ago. They're gone already?"

"I'm here for a very important event." She looked outside the bakery, and her face brightened.

My mother, Austin's parents, and Austin were on their way into the shop. He carried a large tray covered with fabric.

Did he bring them here to show them around? Why hadn't he informed me?

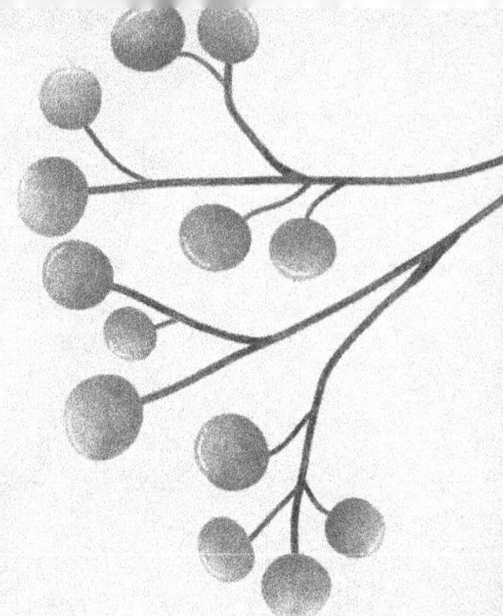

CHAPTER EIGHTEEN

AUSTIN

INSIDE THE BAKERY, Ava's mom and my parents chatted with Ava while I placed the tray on the side table. I spent the morning with them, preparing for this monumental moment. My heart raced with excitement and fear as I studied the woman I love.

"I thought you were heading to Julie's today?" Ava offered her mom a hug.

"We moved it to tomorrow," replied Mrs. Chapman. She had a long conversation with me, making sure I would take care of Ava. She didn't need to worry about that. I planned on making Ava's dreams come true.

"Look!" Her mom showed off the emerald bracelet. "It's so beautiful."

"You deserve it." Her mom kissed her forehead.

"We love your animal bread, Ava! You're so talented!" My mom embraced her, followed by my dad.

"Thank you," Ava said, looking overwhelmed by the sudden arrival of family and friends.

Her cheerful friends entered, joining Kendra, who pulled out her phone to show them something.

"What are you guys doing here?" Ava walked over to Rhea, Layla, Jemma, and Deidre.

"We heard great things about the shop, so we decided to pop in." Rhea smiled, looked over at me and winked. I'd asked for her help in inviting the girls here today.

After giving her friends a hug, Ava slid me a glance full of questions. She knew something was up when Bianca entered, greeted everyone, and flipped the open sign to closed.

"What is going on?"

Ava whirled to me to see me holding the tray of baked goods, and I said, "For you."

"Oh my gosh." Ava picked up the cat-shaped bread and read the notecard out loud. "*I loaf you meow and forever.*"

"I loaf you too," I replied.

Our small audience giggled.

"Aren't they cute?" Ava's mom clasped her hands together, looking happy.

Ava placed the bread down and grabbed a muffin with marshmallow eyes. She smiled and read the card. "*Muffin compares to your beautiful buns.*"

"Sign me up for the X-rated baked goods!" Kendra raised her hand, laughing.

"Did you not see the big warning: DO NOT EAT?" Rhea exclaimed.

"Don't eat it," said my mother, who had tasted one bun earlier.

Everyone laughed, including Ava, who continued to review all the baked goods. Some looked decent and some needed a little imagination.

She turned to me with love in her eyes. "You're so creative."

"I learned from the best."

Ava grabbed the card from the heart-shaped bread. "*Love is what the heart kneads.*" Tears glimmered in her eyes.

With my heart hammering in my chest, I dropped to one knee. "I love you, Ava. You're the best bun in my bakery."

Laughter filled the store like a sweet aroma. With gleaming eyes, Ava grinned and placed a hand on her heart.

"Will you give me the honor of baking happiness with you?" I said, knowing I sounded cheesy, but I didn't care. Ava would appreciate it. "Will you marry me?" I pulled out the ring she had tried on and loved at Annette's Jewelry.

"Yes, yes, yes—you silly and creative man!" she exclaimed.

I slid the gold ring with the solitaire diamond onto her finger and rose to a standing position.

She glanced at the ring, and more tears slid down her face. "It's perfect, and it fits!" She threw her arms around me, kissed me, and veered back. "You planned all this?"

"He did!" the crowd announced together.

"He's a keeper!" Rhea shouted.

"Since all the people I love are here, I've got an announcement to make." She intertwined her fingers with mine. "No Name needs a new name to celebrate a new beginning."

I'd been waiting to hear what she'd call it.

"What is it?" Cindy exclaimed.

"Beautiful Buns." She looked up at me and offered a smile laced with mischief and amusement.

I love my wicked fiancée and her creative mind.

"Oh my god!" Layla laughed.

"You guys are so pervy!" Kendra exclaimed.

"You're thinking all the wrong things." Ava gestured to her display of animal breads. "Aren't these beautiful buns?"

"They are, sweetheart." My mom offered me support with a wink. Then her face softened. "Your father would be so proud of you."

"I know he's watching over me." Ava dabbed tears from her eyes.

"I love it," Jemma said. "The name is up for interpretation, and that's the beauty of it."

Donna and Cindy walked around with trays of bread and pastries for everyone while Bianca and Rosie set out the drinks.

Kendra chose a cat bun with a small face and an adorable butt and tail.

"Beautiful buns, indeed." She giggled as she squeezed the sweet bread with her fingers, making her friends laugh.

Ava and I stood watching our friends and family having a good time. When no one was watching, I cupped my fiancée's ass and whispered, "These beautiful buns are mine. Can't wait to explore them tonight."

"Same here." Her cheeks blossomed, making me the happiest man in the world.

EPILOGUE

SIX MONTHS *later*

Ava

I never imagined my life would be filled with so much joy, but here I was living out my spectacular dreams. Sierra and her family were on trial for a long list of crimes. Austin and I had a small wedding in January and enjoyed our honeymoon in Paris.

I'd resigned from my city job and now dedicated myself to Beautiful Buns, creating more unique pastries and bread. We added a new addition to the store, allowing for more tables and chairs and a party room. Paula had returned and resumed her baking duties. We also hired two new employees, one of whom managed our marketing campaigns.

I prepared one last platter of animal-shaped bread for a

little girl's birthday party. "This is ready for Francesca Lombardo."

"Are you okay?" Cindy asked. "You look pale."

"I'm heading home early. Been working too much."

"We know." Cindy smiled. "Go home. We've got it here."

I grabbed my purse and started out when a family strode in. I sneezed as Juan approached.

"Bless you," he said.

"Thank you," I said to the man who had stolen my emerald bracelet. I'd heard from Officer Jensen that he'd finished his community service early.

"Hi." I smiled. "How are you?"

"Because of you, I'm good. This is my family." He gestured to a lovely woman in a floral dress. "My wife, Carla, and daughter, Joelle." His daughter looked healthy and happy in her Hello Kitty T-shirt and jeans.

"Thank you for giving him a chance," Carla said with tears filling her eyes. "You saved our family." She draped an arm around her daughter. "Joelle has recovered wonderfully, thanks to your husband."

Austin?

"Oh, what did he do?"

Juan smiled. "He paid for Joelle's medical services—all of them."

My chest constricted. I had no idea Austin had done that. I loved that man more each day.

"Thank you for helping me." Joelle walked up, hugging me.

I embraced her back. "I'm so happy you're healed. Live life to the fullest, and listen to your parents, okay?"

"Okay." She beamed. "We're here to support you. I love pastries."

While Carla and Joelle browsed, Juan told me, "I got a new job that has better health insurance now."

"That's wonderful news!" I cheered.

"I'm part of the maintenance team at Austin's new property in Auburn. It's about a ten-minute drive from home. Thank you for *everything*." He reached for my hand and shook it. "I'm so grateful."

"You're welcome."

My heart was full when I arrived home. Who knew Juan's life would turn out so beautifully. He'd made a mistake because of his love for his daughter. Everyone deserved a second chance.

Feeling overly sensitive, I poured myself a glass of juice and sat on the couch in the living room, crying.

When Austin arrived home, he saw me and rushed over. "What's wrong?"

Austin

"Just happy." She stretched out her arms to me.

Coming home and seeing her everyday was a blessing. When Jeremy told me Sierra had targeted Ava, I was ready to release my evidence. But I didn't need to anymore because other victims had come forward with more proof that would put the Montage family in prison for a long time.

"Happy tears?" I wrapped an arm around her. "Tell me what I missed."

I was worried she'd been working too much. She'd looked pale for a few weeks now. I'd told her to cut back her hours at the bakery, but she refused. The joy on her face when people bought her creations was indescribable.

"Juan stopped by the shop today with his family. He told me what you did." She cupped my face with both hands and kissed me. "Why didn't you tell me?"

I shrugged. "You were busy fulfilling orders. He mentioned he'd stop by with his family to thank you."

"You're now his boss." Ava leaned back onto the couch, sounding out of breath. "You gave them a miracle."

"You were my miracle when you came back to me." I squeezed her shoulder. "So it makes sense to share the magic with others."

She told me about Carla buying two boxes of pastries to share with their friends.

Ava shifted to face me. "I've got a miracle for you."

"Yeah? An evening date baking in the kitchen with you in sexy lingerie?"

"Maybe." She laughed. "I've got a bun in the oven."

"What are you baking?" I looked toward the kitchen. "I don't smell anything."

She took my hand and placed it over her belly. "This kind of bun."

Unspeakable joy burst in my belly. "Really?" I rubbed her flat stomach.

"I found out last week." Excitement filled her eyes. "Haven't told anyone yet."

I kissed her and understood why she'd felt tired. Excitement, worry, and happiness coursed through me.

"We both 'kneaded' love." I smiled at my gorgeous wife

as I gave her belly a light squeeze. "And that created our little bun."

Laughing, she kissed me. "Never gonna get bored of these puns."

"We can open a sister store and call it Buns and Puns. We can add a bookstore to it." I kissed her neck. "Maybe this is an opportunity for your collection of edible wearables for lovers." Our honeymoon flashed into my mind. "We can repeat what happened in Paris."

"Not a bad idea at all." She giggled.

Grateful for this new addition to our family, we spent the rest of the day exploring baby names. My family was growing, and I was a blessed man excited to meet my son or daughter.

Thank you so much for reading!

Read the next book, **The Cursed Holiday Card!**

If you enjoyed Season of Kneading Love, I'd truly appreciate it if you could leave a review on your chosen platform(s). Every review counts. Thank you!

Here's the bonus scene, HONEYMOON IN PARIS, for you!

Check out my other books!

The Mastermind
The Daredevil
The Innovator
The Inquisitor
The Strategist
The Protege
The Maverick
Etched in Ink
Finding Your HeART

www.nadiahan.com

ACKNOWLEDGMENTS

Thank you to my family for loving me and everything I do. Thank you to my editors, beta readers, proofreaders, and the ARC team for helping me make this story the best it can be. I can never forget my lovely readers for reading my work and inspiring me to write more books. You guys are the best buns in town!

Nadia Han is a contemporary romance author. She's a dreamer, a visionary, and a believer in karma and kindness. She lives in Massachusetts with her husband, two children, and a cat, and enjoys the unpredictable New England weather.

Nadia started out writing and illustrating children's books when her kids were small. But she decided to write romantic suspense stories featuring diverse characters for herself. She loves escaping into different worlds and for that reason, she also writes otherworldly romance under a different pen name.

When she's not writing, she practices yoga, reads, explores nature, watches K-dramas, and eats all kinds of foods. Nadia is also an artist. She loves spending time playing with paint and other artistic mediums. She believes creativity is important for the mind and the soul. It helps her become a better writer because she can guide the reader to see things from a different perspective.

f facebook.com/authornadiahan

O instagram.com/authornadiahan

BB bookbub.com/authors/nadia-han

a amazon.com/author/nadiahan